REDSKIN RAIDERS ON THE GALACTIC RIM

Kade Whitehawk had two strikes against him in the Space Service. First, he had bungled his assignment on the planet Lodi. Second, he believed all creatures had a right to freedom and dignity—and having such opinions was strictly against the rules.

But when he was assigned to Klor, he found the Ikkinni there—tortured yet defiant slaves of a vicious tyrant race.

Right then Kade swung at the last pitch. For rules or no rules, THE SIOUX SPACEMAN knew that he had to help these strange creatures gain their freedom . . . and that he alone, because of his Indian blood, had the key to win it for them.

THE SIOUX SPACEMAN

by

ANDRE NORTON

ACE BOOKS, INC.

1120 Avenue of The Americas
New York, N.Y. 10036

THE SIOUX SPACEMAN

Copyright ©, 1960, by Ace Books, Inc.

All Rights Reserved

CHAPTER 1

ON LODI, a crossroad station of the space lanes, the Outworld Traders Base had been set up to accommodate transient servicemen on their way to and from assignments. It had the calculated comfort of a leave post, combined with the impersonality of a space port caravansary, that very impersonality a goad to flight if one had an uneasy conscience.

In the reception lounge of the assignment officer, a young man was seated in an easy rest which embraced his lanky body with an invitation to relaxation he plainly did not accept. One brown hand moved across the breast of his garnet red dress tunic. A twinge of pain followed that faint pressure. He would carry more than one scar for the rest of his life reminding him of his failure at his first post.

Only a stubborn spark of rebellion far inside Kade Whitehawk still insisted that he had been right. He frowned at a wall he did not see and freed himself from the foam cushion with a twist of his shoulders, planted his boots squarely on the floor, again baffled by a contradiction he had been facing for days. Why *had* the Service tests assigned him to outpost duty when he manifestly could not emotionally adjust to meeting Styor arrogance with the necessary detachment and control?

Service tests were supposed to be above question, always fitting the right man to the right job. Then why hadn't it been clear that one Kade Whitehawk, Amerindian of the Northwest Terran Confederation, under the right provocation would revert with whirlwind action to less diplomatic practices of savage ancestors and handle a Styor lordling just as that alien's decadent cruelty demanded?

What if the tests were not infallable? Blind faith in them

5

was a part of the creed of the Service. And if the tests could so misfire, what about the sacrosanct Policy?

Kade's hand balled to a fist on his knee. That Policy of neutral coexistence with the Styor rasped, or should rasp, every Terran. Suppose one could challenge the Policy, upset the Styor rule somewhere along the Star lanes and make it stick! Given a chance at the right time—

"Whitehawk!" The metallic voice of the call-box hissed the whisper through the lounge. He stood up, jerked his tunic smooth, and tramped into the next room to face a man who displayed no signs of welcome.

"Whitehawk reporting, sir."

Ristoff regarded his subordinate with detachment, his broad face impassive. Just so did Kade's own tribal elders confront an offender.

"You realize, of course, that your recent actions have thrown grave doubt on your eligibility for reassignment?"

"Yes, sir."

But I wouldn't have been called here, Kade thought, if that first official verdict had not been set aside. I'd already have been shipped out on the transport which lifted for home yesterday. Which means something has changed!

"We can not prevent the rising of emergencies." Dislike, cold and deadly, underlay those formal words. "And sometimes our hand is forced. A mixed Team on Klor has just lost one of its members by an act of violence. As you are the only one of your race unattached on Lodi at the moment, we are obliged to send you. You understand that this is a concession almost without precedent, considering the charge against you, Whitehawk, and that any future mark on your record will mean immediate dismissal, perhaps further proceedings under our charter?"

"Yes, sir."

Mixed Team! That was a jolt. Mixed Teams were special. Why, with his record smeared apparently past redemption, had he been given a mixed Team status, even temporarily?

"You will ship out at fourteen hours on the *Marco Polo*, with a personal kit not to exceed one shoulder bag. The Team has been established dirt-side five months now and are fully supplied. And, Whitehawk, just one more mistake and it may mean the labor gangs for you."

"Yes, sir."

Of course, mixed Team work was dangerous. Kade wondered if they used such duty as a form of discipline now and then. Exile and possible execution in one? No, Team responsibilities were too important to suggest they were a disposal for the unwanted. Mixed Teams were sent to open up trade on those primitive planets ruled, but not colonized, by the Styor; undeveloped worlds with native races held in peonage by the alien lords.

Kade thought about the Styor as he sorted gear in his quarters, trying to be objective, not influenced by his personal dislike for the aliens. Physically they were humanoid enough to pass at least as cousins of the Terrans. Mentally and emotionally the two species were parsecs apart. The Styor had built their star empire long ago. Now it was beginning to crack a little at the seams. However, they still had galactic armadas able to reduce an enemy planet to a cinder, and they dominated two-thirds of the inhabited and inhabitable worlds.

So far their might could not be challenged by the League. Thus there was an uneasy truce, the Policy, and trade. Traders went where the Patrol of the League could not diplomatically venture. In the beginning of Terran galactic expansion some Styor lords had attempted to profit by that fact. Traders had died in slave pens, been killed in other various unpleasant ways. But the response of the Service had been swift and effective. Trade with the offending lord, planet or system had been cut off. And the Styor found themselves without luxuries and products which had become necessities. Exploiting the wealth of worlds, they needed trade to keep from stagnating, and to bolster up their economic structure—the Styor themselves now considering such an occupation below their own allowed employments of politics and war—and the Terrans were there to be used.

With an inborn belief in their godship, and weapons superior to any possessed by the Terran upstarts, the Styor continued their empire. Styor lords dealt with any rebellion by a subject race drastically. Believing themselves invincible, they tolerated the Terrans.

But fire smoldered, never quite dying into ashes. Let one subject world make a successful resistance—Kade detoured about a mound of crates on his way to the ship pickup platform. He caught the pungent reek of animal odor and glanced at the contents of the nearest, making out a furred ball three-quarters buried in soft-pack. The prisoner of the cage had already been needled into sleep for the take-off, but it was plainly live cargo, and Kade was surprised. Not many shippers could afford the high rates for animal cartage across the star lanes.

Aboard the *Marco Polo* he found his own cramped cabin, endured the discomfort of take-off impatiently. When free to shuck his acceleration straps, he reached eagerly for the portable tape reader which could supply him with all the Terran information on Klor.

The instructive sequence of pictures crossing the palm-sized screen absorbed him. This was an encyclopedia of knowledge stripped to the essentials. As he studied, Kade was teased by an odd sense that something in this combination of history, geography and trade lore was hauntingly familiar. But he could not single out any fact he was sure he had known before.

Along his spine crept that chill which warns the fighting man of an ambush ahead, one no other sense has disclosed. Yet there was nothing more dangerous on Klor, as far as these records went, than on half a dozen other frontier worlds he could name.

The man whose place he was filling—how had Rostoff put it?—"Lost by an act of violence." Kade considered those stilted words. Had the Styor played one of their old tricks? No, a Terran's death at the hands of the Styor could not have been kept a secret, in spite of all hush-hush precautions. Such a rumor would have spread with speed across the whole Lodi base. Act of violence did not mean accident either.

Klor: climate in the temperate zones similar to that of northern Terran continents; three land masses, two lying north and south of the equator in the western hemisphere, and one, long, narrow, shaped roughly like a hook, occupying both hemispheres in the east. The south-western continent was so twisted by volcanic action that the land mass was largely a waterless, uninhabited desert, having no assets to attract the Styor. A handful of squalid native fishing villages clung tenaciously to its northern tip.

The hook land of the east was the most important to the Traders. Though there was a spine of sharply set peaks running diagonally the length of the continent and those peaks conventionally equipped with a fringe of foothills, the major portion of the land consisted of grassed plains. In fact, that section bore a fleeting resemblance to the ancient maps of his own home before the atomic wars had ended one civilization and allowed the return of his own race from backwaters of desert and mountain land where they had been driven earlier by the encroachment of a mechanized culture which had at last blown itself out of existence. The plains of Klor stirred ancient racial memories in Kade.

About halfway down the spine of the main mountain range, but set in the level country, was the Terran Trade Post. Its site marked a mid-point between the two major Styor centers. One housed the giant smelter-producer of kamstine, the other, Cor, the administrative headquarters for the whole planet. The rest of the country was carved into strips and patches which were the individual holdings of the lords. But Klor, except for the mines which were counted as personal holdings of the Emperor, was not rich picking. With the possible exception of the High-Lord-Pac, the aliens in residence on this frontier planet would be men of new families, or failures sent into limbo by clan exile, men under a cloud at home.

Terra's import was not kamstine, they had no use for the stuff, but fur. Those jagged mountains, showing their dull gray rock bones through patches of ochre vegetation, were honeycombed with caves, and most of those caves harbored musti in seemingly inexhaustable flocks.

There were bats of Terra whose silver-silk fur, had it been in sizeable skins, would have excited the trades with their beauty. But a pelt only fingers wide had no value. Man prospected the stars before he discovered the musti. Like the bats of his home world, the leather-winged flyers of Klor were nocturnal, but their wings had a spread of ten feet and the furred bodies they supported were in proportion. The fur was silky, with a delicate ripple-wave, or, as with the musti of the upper heights, a short spring-curl, shaded in color from the silver-grey of Klorian rock to the dark blue of her night sky. And one season's catch could raise the leave-pension bonus of a Trader to an upper-bracket income.

Musti were hunted by the Ikkinni, the natives. Each Styor lord had as many Ikkinni slaves as he could capture in the mountains or buy from a professional slaver. Kade pressed the repeat button on the reader, studied the image which appeared on the screen.

Humanoid, yes—but certainly X-Tee—although more alien physically than the Styor who argued by that premise that the Ikkinni were mere animals. And certainly in contrast to their oppressors they were weirdly different.

The specimen on the viewer was perhaps Kade's height, but the length and slenderness of arms and legs gave an illusion of added inches. Body and limbs were covered with fine, long black hair through which white skin showed pallidly. The hair was heavier on shoulders and chest, rising on top of the head into a peak of coarser, stiffer growth. On the cheeks and chin the sprouting was a soft down from which a hard beak of nose protruded in a bold curve, overshadowing the rest of the features. A wide, seemingly lipless mouth was a little open, and teeth, certainly those of a carnivore, matched the skin in whiteness.

For clothing the native wore a sash-like length about the hips, the ends brought between the legs and drawn through the front band, to hang free to knee level, the material a tanned hide. But the collar about the native's neck proclaimed his slave status.

About three inches wide, that article fitted smoothly to the flesh, and Kade knew that its presence doomed the unfortunate Ikkinni to the lifelong servitude from the moment it was welded on. For that band was a guard, a taskmaster, a punishment in turn, by the whim of the Styor owner. Impulses broadcast miles away could transmit jolts of pain, or killing agony, to the slave. One could not escape by running.

Before the coming of the Styor, as far as the Terrans could learn, the Ikkinni had lived in loosely governed tribes, mostly in collections of two or more family clans. Intertribal war had existed, usually as a means of obtaining new wives or raising the prestige of the competing tribes. They had been wandering hunters, with the exception of some coastal fishermen and a handful of families who had settled in the highly fertile river bottoms to plant and harvest fruit and grain.

The farmers had been the first victims of the Styor aggression, the hunters retreating after a series of disasterous skirmishes into the mountains where freak air currents prevented the use of Styor aircraft. Slavers still led raids into those vast mountains and trapped Ikkinni with the same dispatch as the natives in turn netted the musti of the caves.

Kade noted the two spears and coiled net that the primitive in the tape scene carried. They were no defense against a blaster, a needler, or the supposedly innocuous stunner allowed Terran Traders on Styor-held worlds. And without any effective weapon, what chance had the poor devils ever had?

The Terran's hand had gone to the grip of the weapon riding on his own hip before he realized where that line of thought led. Tadder could happen all over again. He was thinking in the same pattern which had led to his disgrace there. Traders did not meddle. At the slightest hint of any involvement with local affairs outside the strict bounds of the service duties, their commanding officer shipped them back to base. He must remember. Remember and control his temper and instincts.

Kade adjusted the reader, called into being on its screen the list of Team personnel. Not that he could hope for any backing from those veterans if he blasted off orbit a second time.

"Shaka Abu, Commander." The click of words introduced his new superior officer. An Africo-Venusian, tough-looking, the slightest tinge of gray showing in his head lock. Perhaps not a particularly successful man or he wouldn't still be a Team leader in the field, but rather would occupy some position of greater authority at one of the sector bases.

"Che'in Lan." Younger, placid, something self-satisfied in his sleepy-eyed face.

"Jon Steel."

Kade curbed a start of surprise as he viewed the picture of not just a fellow Amerindian, but one, by the faint touch of paint between his brows, of the Lakota; a tribesman of the Sioux! This must be the man he replaced, the one who had died by violence. No Team had more than one representative of any Terran race.

"Manuel Santoz." Kade hardly glanced at the last man on the list. He was too intent on Jon Steel, who had died on Klor. Again that sensation of a waiting trap. There were too many coincidences in all this.

Sure, many Armerindians were enlisted in the Service, the adventure of out-world duty was welcomed by the youth of the Federation of Tribes. But there were twenty or more of those tribes with numerous subdivisions. For a Lakota to replace a Lakota seemed hardly to come about by chance alone.

And Ristoff, because of his position, must have known that to send Kade to take the place of a dead tribal brother was to unleash an avenger. Or was this sequence of events a new and stiffer testing set up on purpose? If Kade followed the dictates of tribal custom and made trouble on Klor, then Ristoff would have him, space cold.

He slid his stunner from its holster, checked the charge now activating that side arm. The weapon could not kill, not with the diluted energy issued to Trade men, but it could knock an enemy insensible, to be dealt with in a more fatal fashion when and if opportunity offered.

However Kade had learned one lesson on Tadder; the need for caution. In the old, old days his kind had had a standard to measure skill and courage. One entered a hostile camp and exited again unharmed, undetected, bringing along an enemy's favorite war mount into the bargain. He'd play his own game. If Ristoff had set up a frame for some murky reason, he'd learn the why of that, too. Again there was that chill along his back, almost as if a coup stick had thudded home. And not a friendly one, no, not a friendly one at all!

When the *Marco Polo* broke out of hyper over Klor, Kade knew all the Terran records could tell him about that world. He could trace an accurate course from the most detailed maps available to the Traders, which included the musti hunting grounds in the mountains. For the Styor allowed hunting passes for periodic inspection of the trapped caves, to make certain that one section was not being denuded of breeding-stock. Such details were beneath the attention of the local lordling whose income might depend upon the result of a season's net work in the caverns.

In addition, the Terran had added to his storehouse of facts all points dealing with the Ikkinni, although limited, since the Styor did *not* encourage any anthropological research on the part of off-worlders. And he had tabulated his own findings concerning the methods and manners of the Styor, together with any modifications of those as listed by Terran observation on Klor. He had no idea of what lay ahead, save that the problem of Jon Steel's death was part of it. But in some way the doubts he had had in the waiting lounge on Lodi were backing his determination to do some investigating on his own.

He might have guessed that that was not going to be too easy, Kade thought a twenty-seven hour day later when he did at last have a measure of privacy. With a small staff, every member of the Team had been engaged in high-pressure work seeing to the disposition of the *Marco Polo's* cargo and the mountain of paper work to be discharged before the transport lifted again. Kade, with only hasty introductions to his fellows, had been so buried in details that after a full day and night on Klor, he still had only a confused impression of post and personnel.

There were Ikkinni porters in service, hired out from their Styor masters. And one of them now stood just within the door panel of Kade's room, his eyes with their ruddy pupils gathering extra fire from the atom lamp, his long fingers hooked into the front of his sash kilt.

"It wants?" Kade asked in the tongue he had learned as well as he could from the Hypo-trainer on ship board.

"It has." The Ikkinni reached back a foot, hooked limber toes about a package and pushed it from corridor to room, showing the usual reluctance of his people to the carrying of burdens. A Styor would have instantly punished that act of rebellion. Kade made no show of knowing the subtle defiance for what it was.

Neither did he move to pick up the packet, knowing that to do so would be to admit inferiority.

"It has where?" He looked carefully beyond the packet lying on the floor. Then, turning his back to the native, he busied himself with placing a pile of record tapes in a holder.

"It has here."

Kade glanced around. The packet now rested on his bunk. Since no one had witnessed the action which had put it there, honor on both sides had been maintained.

"It has my thanks for its courtesy." Deliberately the Terran used the warrior intonation.

Those red eyes met his. There was no change of expression which Kade could read on that down-covered face. With a quick movement the native disappeared through the half-open panel of the door. He might never have been there, save that the packet was on the bunk. Kade picked it up, read the official markings of the Research and Archives Division. Below them was a name; STEEL.

For a long moment he weighed the package in his hand. But the communication was not personal. And officially the contents might well be his business. He smothered a small twinge of guilt and stripped away the wrapping, eager to discover what had been so important that Jon Steel had sent to Base for aid.

CHAPTER 2

Sample submitted has the following properties, Kade read in the code-script of the Service. There was a listing of chemical symbols. *It will therefore ably nourish and support Terran herbivores without difficulty, being close in structure to the grama grass of our western continental plains.*

Grama grass, suitable nourishment for Terran herbivores—Kade read the symbols a second time and then studied in turn the two accompanying enclosures, each sheathed in a plasta-protector. Both were whisps, perhaps a finger long, of dried vegetation carrying a seed head. One was a palish gray-brown. It could represent a tuft of Terran hay. The other was much darker, a dull, rusty red, and Kade thought it might have been pulled from roots in the plain now stretching away beyond the outer wall of the Klorian post.

So, Steel had sent a selection of native grass to be analyzed. And, judging by the wording of this report, analyzed with a purpose in mind, to see if it could nourish some form of Terran animal life. Why?

Kade pulled down one of the wall-slung seats and sat before the desk, laying the grass on its surface. He knew this must be important. Important enough to be paid for by a man's life? Or did the report have anything at all to do with Steel's death? And how *had* he died? So far, none of the men Kade had met here had mentioned his predecessor. He must get access to Steel's report tapes, discover why a finger-thick roll of Klorian wild grass had been sent to Prime Base for analytical processing.

The clear chime of the mess call sounded and Kade unsealed his tunic, tucking the contents of the packet into his inner valuables belt for the safest keeping he knew.

To join any established Team was never easy for the newcomer. In addition Kade knew that Abu had been duly warned concerning his glaring misdeed of the immediate past. He would need strong self-control and his wits to last out the probationary period the others would put him through. And, had he not had this private mystery to chew upon, he might have dreaded his first session with his new Teammates more.

But there was no outward strain in the mess hall where the odors of several exotic dishes mingled. Each man ate rather absently while he dealt with his own newly arrived pile of private message flimsies, catching up with the concerns off Klor which had meaning for him. And Kade was free to study the assortment of Terrans without having to be too subtle in appraisement.

Commander Abu ate stolidly, as an engine might refuel, his attention held by the reader through which a united strip of flimsies crawled at a pace which suggested that either the Team leader was not a swift-sighter, or else that there was enough solid meat in his messages to entail complete concentration.

On the other hand, Che'in's round face betrayed a variety of fleeting emotions with the mobility of a Tri-Vee actor as one flimsy after another flicked in and out of his reader. Now and then he clucked indignantly, made a sound approaching a glutton's lip-smacking, or chuckled, entering all the way into the spirit of his personal mail.

The third man, Santoz, had yet another method. Reading a flimsy selected from one pile before him, he would detach it from his machine, place it on a second heap, and stare at the wall while he chewed and swallowed several mouthfuls before beginning the process all over again. Kade was trying to deduce character traits from the actions of his three tablemates when one of the Ikkinni materialized by the door. Without turning his head Abu asked in the Trade speech:

"It comes. Why?"

"It has concern." But no inflection of that slurred speech suggested great emotion.

"It has concern. Why?"

"The furred thing from the stars cries aloud."

Abu looked at Kade. "This comes under your department, Whitehawk. I understand you have had vet training. That bear is important to our relations with the High-Lord-Pac. Better take a look right away."

Kade followed the native to the courtyard, close to the smaller warehouse where the more valuable trade articles were stored. Now he could hear the whining snuffle of his patient. The cage crate he had seen ready to be loaded at Lodi stood here under the protecting overhang of the warehouse roof, and its inhabitant was not only awake but distinctly unhappy.

The Terran squatted on his heels before the cage to see that the captive was indeed a Terran bear, about half grown, a white collar of fur across the chest showing in contrast to the rest of a dark pelt now linted with whisps of protective bedding.

Any bear shipped off-world would have come from one of the special breeding farms, the docile descendent of generations that had lived with mankind and been domesticated to such cohabitation. But no space trip, even taken in a drugged state, could have left the animal anything but nervous. And the captaive in the cage was decidedly woebegone.

At Kade's soothing hiss the animal crowded closer to the restraining bars, peered at him, and uttered a whine, low pitched and coaxing.

The Trader read the label sealed to the top of the shipping cage. The bear was consigned to the High-Lord Pac himself. No wonder it was necessary to see that such an astronomically expensive shipment arrived in the best condition. Kade fingered the lock, eased the front to the pavement of the courtyard. He heard a stir behind him, guessed the Ikkinni had lingered to watch.

Would the distinctive, strange body odor of the native have any effect on the bear? Kade motioned with one hand, hoping that the Ikkinni could properly interpret the order to withdraw.

Even though the cage was now open, the bear hesitated, pacing back and forth as if still facing a barrier, and whined.

"Come, boy. Soooo. There is nothing to be afraid of," Kade coaxed. He held out his hand, not to touch but to be touched, to have that black button of a nose sniff inquiringly along his fingers, across the back of his hand, up his arm, as the bear, as if pulled by a familiar scent, came out of the cage.

Then, with a sudden rush, the animal bumped against Kade, sending the man sprawling backward as the round head drove against his chest with force enough to bring a grunt of protest out of him. The Terran's hands went to the bear's ears as the moist nose, a rough tongue met his chin.

"Now, boy, take it easy! You're all right."

The man squirmed free of that half embrace, found himself sitting on the pavement with three-quarters of a heavy body resting on his thighs. Then he laughed and scratched behind the rounded ears. There was nothing wrong with this particular specimen of Terran wildlife except loneliness and fear. He fondled the bear and spoke to the hovering Ikkinni.

"Has the furred one from the stars eaten?"

"It gave the furred one food. But the furred one did not eat."

"Bring the food again."

Kade sat on the stone watching the round head bob, listening to the slurp of food disappearing as the bear now greedily dug into the contents of a bowl.

"The furred one wears no collar."

Kade glanced up. The Ikkinni's right fingers swept along his own haired shoulder inches away from the badge of his slave state.

"Only the one it was born with." Kade touched the white markings on the bear's dark coat.

"Yet the furred one obeys—"

The Terran understood the puzzlement behind the other's half-question. There were animals in plenty beside the musti known to the natives of Klor, but none were domesticated. To the Ikkinni a beast was either to be hunted for food, fought for protection, or without value at all, and so to be ignored. There were no dogs on Klor, no cats to guard a hearth, no horses—

No horses! Kade's mind caught at that, a faint glimmer, something—but he had no time to pursue it. Abu came across the courtyard.

"Everything all right?"

"Yes. Just a case of homesickness, I would say." The younger man got to his feet and the Ikkinni faded out of sight. Having finished licking his supper bowl the bear sat back on his haunches, rocking a little, round nose up to test new scents.

"What's a bear doing here anyway?" Kade asked.

"A new toy," the Commander snorted. "The High-Lord-Pac Scarkan is organizing a private zoo. It was Steel's project. He brought an assortment of animal tri-dee shots and showed them to Scarkan the last time he went to Cor for permit renewal. New things always enchant the Styor, but the enthusiasm probably won't last, it seldom does." Abu regarded his new Team recruit shrewdly, "Unless you can keep him stirred up to want some more. We won't transport elephants, remember. And no animal that can not adapt to Klor."

The report on the grass made sense now. Steel had had another sale in mind when he had asked for that. Deer? Cattle? Some animal decorative enough to hold jaded Styor interest.

"If I could see his report tape," Kade ventured.

"There's one thing, Whitehawk. If you do deal directly with the Styor—" The Commander left that sentence hanging unfinished though Kade could provide the missing words. Dealing with the Styor, considering his past record, might be out of the question. He shrugged.

"You said it yourself, Commander, animals have been my special training. I can work up the sales pitch, let someone else deliver it."

Abu unfroze. "Fair enough. And, since animals are your business, you'd better take trap duty on the next expedition. Give you the lay of the land and break you in at that same time. Come along."

When Kade followed, the bear shuffled behind him. Abu glanced around once but did not suggest that the cage was a more fitting place than the corner of the room into which he led the younger man. Then both forget the animal as they turned to the maps on the walls.

"We lease our hunting teams from three different lords. It makes for competition and prevents any monoply of funds. And we rotate leases every other year, which spreads the credit around even farther. The locals may growl about the system, but the High-Lord-Pac agrees. He gets his cut as export duty regardless, and he doesn't want any other lord getting too prosperous."

"Some local trouble?"

"No more than usual. They're always trying to build up their own blast power at the expense of their neighbors. This is a scrap world where every district lord dreams of making a good run so he can emigrate into a bigger game elsewhere. It's the High-Lord-Pac's duty to keep the winnings fairly even —or that's the idea. Sometimes the scheme doesn't work. But so far on Klor there've been no favorites. Anyway, we take the hunting teams out in rotation, and Smohallo's is next. He's got a head tracker who's really expert, an Ikkinni of the Cliffs—"

"A *live* one!" Kade recalled his indoctrination on the *Marco Polo*. Of all the free natives on Klor the Cliff colonies of the highest and least accessible mountains were the hardest to enslave and had offered the Styor the most cunning and effective resistence.

"Yes, a live one. And Smohallo knows his value too. He's been offered what is equivalent to a small fortune for the fellow. Anyway, he put a double thick collar on the poor brute, and so is safe in working him even in the outback. He has a breed from Tadder for his Overman." Abu pulled at his long upper lip with thumb and forefinger. "Lik's a nasty blot on the landscape, but he's Smohallo's right hand and probably about two fingers on the left into the bargain. You'll remember that, Whitehawk."

The words were not a threat, just a stern reminder of fact, a fact which Kade must swallow. His outbreak on Tadder would undoubtedly continue to follow him for years to come.

"I'll remember," he replied shortly.

"So there'll be this tracker, Lik, and six net men, all from Smohallo's estate. You'll take one Ikkinni from here as carrier. Keep clear of Lik. He knows that the count sheet is your work, but because you're new, he may try to run in some half-growns."

Kade nodded. An old practice. To befool the Terrans was the hope of every Styor employee, openly expressed, of every Styor Lord, not so publicly admitted.

"You'll try new ground up north, into this district," Abu traced a map route with the nail of one dark finger. "Lik'll have a sonic which will ward off any attack by lurkers or animals. You may run into a slaver up there. If so, keep your eyes and ears shut and look the other way, understand me!"

"Yes." But he didn't have to pretend to like it, Kade added silently.

"They may be in tomorrow. In the meantime," the Commander went to a file, brought out a disc of tape. "Here's Steel's report. If you can get any ideas from it, they'll be welcome." It was plainly a dismissal but Kade did not leave. Tossing the disc from one hand to the other he looked straight into the harsh face of the other man.

"How did Steel die?"

"With a spear through his middle." The answer was curt.

"Wild Ikkinni?"

"It would seem so. He was out on a trapping trip. There is reason to believe that lurkers were in the neighborhood. So we reported officially."

But you don't believe it, Kade returned silently. And you're just as hot about it as any Lakota. He did not say that aloud for he guessed that the Team Commander was walking very quietly and cautiously along a path which might be mined. Every intonation in the other's voice suggested that. Yes, there was something wrong on Klor, and more than just the usual brutality and tyranny of the Styor.

As he tolled the bear back to its cage, a shadow moved. In the faint reflection of light from a window Kade saw an Ikkinni rise to his feet, wait for the Terran. Perhaps the courtyard watchman.

"It has waited."

"So? Why?" Kade led the bear into its quarters.

22

"To ask why does that animal which wears no collar answer to the words of the starwalker?"

"Because in the world of the Starwalker there is—" Kade sought for a word for friendship, could recall none in the limited trade language and substituted the nearest possible phrase. "There is a common night fire."

The bear whined, pawed at the barrier now between it and Kade. Kade made soothing noises and the animal curled up in the thick bedding.

"A common night fire for starwalker and furred one," the Ikkinni repeated. And then, with apparent irreverence, added, "It is Dokital."

Kade stood still. It took him a second to realize that the native had told him his name. His knowledge of the Ikkinni was limited to what he had learned from tapes. And he didn't know how to interpret this unusual confidence. Now he must feel his way.

"Swift is the spear arm of Dokital," he improvised. "It is Kade." He judged that his first name would mean more to the native.

"There is no spear in its hand," the words poured swiftly from the patch of darkness into which Dokital had stepped. "It wears a collar. It is no longer a man of spears." There was a note in that which brought an instant reaction from Kade.

"Swift is the spear arm of Dokital," he repeated without any emphasis, but firmly. Only that shadow in the shadows was gone. He stood alone by the bear cage.

A shadowy Ikkinni moved through the Terran's dreams that night and he awoke feeling stupid and thick-headed. But he applied himself doggedly to the study of previous trapping reports, striving to add all he could to his general knowledge before he went to the practical testing of the field.

He saw Dokital sweeping in the court, trailing in and out of warehouses pulling the supply carts. However, since the native ignored him, Kade made no move to speak to the other. There were quite a few leased slaves at the post. Kade counted more than a dozen throughout the day, and to them the Terrans paid no attention, except to give an order or two. He did not see any Overman and mentioned that fact to Che'in at lunch.

"Yes, we do not see Buk too often. He has a liking for cabal smoking and so keeps his quarters, except when he gets the signal for a Styor visit here. But that fact works to our advantage. Buk draws his pay and doesn't stir himself, we have no trouble with the Ikkinni, and the Styor get their lease credits on time. What they don't know doesn't hurt. Well—It looks as if I spoke a little too soon. There *is* the post Overman now."

He waved at the viewplate which afforded them a view of the courtyard. A corpulent humanoid, his yellowish skin stretched in a greasy band over a wobbling paunch, was standing beside the bear cage inspecting its occupant in bemused surprise. As all the Overmen, Buk was a half-breed, probably from Yogn, Kade decided. His hairless head had three horn-like bumps across the forehead, and his sharply pointed chin retreated as thick wattle of loose skin into his big neck. His scanty clothing—tight breeches, high boots, loose sleeveless vest—was a travesty of Styor hunting clothes, and he wore the long knife of an underofficer strapped tight to his left thigh. On the whole he was an ugly looking customer, until one saw the slight lurch with which he walked, noted the cloudiness of his pale eyes, and knew he was rotted by cabal addiction—but still to be counted dangerous if he had the advantage in an encounter.

The same gong which usually marked the passing hours at the post now rang a deep toned note and Che'in pushed back his stool.

"Visitors," he informed Kade. "Maybe Smohallo's come along with his gang to see what the *Marco* landed. They're always eager to get something new from off-world to show off first and there's a Dark Time Feast due in about a week where all the local brass will strut."

The Trade Team assembled in the courtyard, wearing red dress tunics, but also stunner clips in their weapons. Out-world Trade was not a collection of natives to be bent to Styor whims. And while the fact was never allowed to come to a test, both sides recognized it.

A second note from the gong was answered by a rasping squall which bit at Terran eardrums. Abu signalled and the force barrier guarding the post flashed off, to disclose an approaching party of some size. The Ikkinni with the nets were, of course, the hunters supplied to the post. Four more slaves pounded along at a trot, carrying on their bent shoulders poles supporting a small platform on which sat cross-legged an Overman who must be Lik. Yes, his big frame and handsome but cruel features were reminiscent of Tadder.

There came a line of Ikkinni bearing burdens, and behind them an elaborate half-curtained carry-chair in which a Styor lounged, his delicate, almost feminine features masked to lip level by a strip of gemed lizard skin which matched the crested headdress he wore. He played with a needler, the most deadly side arm among the stars. His dress was the semi-military one of a reserve soldier though nothing about him suggested that he had ever seen service with the Fleet.

The Ikkinni hunters entered the courtyard, backed against the wall, their chests heaving with the exertion of their pace. Lik arose from the seat and stood watching the Terrans insolently, his thumbs hooked in his belt, his fingers playing about the edge of that control box which could lash out swift pain to any of the collared natives about him.

Abu stepped forward no more than two paces. That, too, was correct. The post was Terra, here Smohallo was a guest and, in a measure, an equal, which fact most of the Styor tried more or less successfully to ignore. Kade, who had been watching the entrance of the local lordling, suddenly noticed a slight movement on Lik's part. He did not quite touch the hilt of his thigh knife, but there was the murderous wish to do so mirrored for a hot instant in his eyes.

And the Tadderan breed had been looking at Kade in that moment. The Terran's own hand dipped so that the grip of his stunner fitted neatly and comfortably into his palm. But that half-challenge occupied less than a second of time. Lik's eyes slid past Kade, were now fixed with wonder on the bear cage.

CHAPTER 3

KADE TOPPED the small rise, stood for a moment in the pull of a wind which held some of the damp breath of peak snow. Ahead the line of Ikkinni hunters trotted, heads down, shoulders hunched, followed by Lik, this time on his own two feet. They were striking up a valley which narrowed into a gorge, a tongue of plains land licking into mountain territory. Another few Terran miles, perhaps by midday, and they would reach the end of the known country, heading into wild lands which had not been before prospected by the musti trappers.

Even in this place the grass growth was calf high. By midseason it should reach well up a man's thigh. The grass equaled the grama covering of the Terran plains. Why had that been so important to Steel? Kade had had no chance to check the other's report tape before leaving the post. But there was one fact he did know, that Steel had been on just such an expedition as this when he had been found with an unidentified Ikkinni spear through him. Only last night Lik had made reference to that happening, had suggested the folly of any Terran leaving the hunting camp or wandering from the party on the march.

"These animals," the Overman had indicated his charges with a hooked thumb. "We can make them squeak to our piping." He patted his belt control. "But the lurkers in the mountains. Unless a man has a sonic, he is easy meat for them, never seeing his death until he has swallowed it."

"I thought all hunting parties were equipped with sonics," Kade observed.

"That is so. But such is the property of the Overman. Should one wander away too far—" Lik made a gesture like a Terran shrugging off the responsibility for such folly.

"I am warned." Kade had kicked his bedroll to the left, well away from Lik's vicinity. As he unsealed his sleeping bag he heard a faint rustle in the grass, guessed rather than saw Dokital had bedded down with the same avoidance of the Overman. Luckily since the Ikkinni was of the post crew Kade was reasonably sure Lik could not cause the young native trouble without his own knowledge and chance to interfere. Dokital's collar had been triggered by Buk against any run for freedom, but he could not be controlled by Lik's box.

Now, the morning after, the native drew even with Kade. Unlike his fellow slaves he held his head up, his eyes were fixed on the mountain peaks glistening white against the clear sky. Kade considered those peaks. There were three, set almost in a straight line, or so it appeared from the point where they now stood. And the Terran noted that their outlines suggested figures: Men, muffled in cloaks, folded in wings? He almost could believe that their party was under observation from that quarter, and for no friendly purpose.

"There is a name?" He nodded to the three sky-crowned giants.

"There are names," Dokital agreed. "Yuma, the Planner, Simc, the Netter, Homc, who strikes with a spear." He shifted the band which held Kade's field kit to his shoulders. "They wait."

"For us?" Kade asked on impulse.

"For that which will be." The Ikkinni's head came down, now aping the dull endurance of his fellows. But Kade had caught that half promise. Or was it a threat?

They camped at noon beside a stream which widdened to pond proportions. A wiry Ikkinni, who had kept well to the fore all morning and who must be Iskug, the cliff man Abu had mentioned, hooked a fish out of the water. The creature was not scaled. Its rough, warty skin resembled that of a Terran toad, but bright red in color, and it had a spiky growth of hard blue mandibles about a narrow snout. Broiled over a fire it smelled far better than it looked and, feeling confidence in his immunity shots, Kade accepted a portion, discovering that the pinkish meat tasted better yet.

The Terran was alert to every sign of animal or bird life about them, making notes on his wrist recorder of two species of grazers they had sighted that morning, one equipped with a nose horn, the other apparently without any form of defense except fleetness. There were rodent things in the grass, and a flightless, feathered bird as fleet as the grazer but twice its size, which Kade was glad had not tried to dispute their passage. The spurs on its huge feet had been warning of a belligerent nature and, when it had opened its bill to squawk at them, he was certain he had sighted serrations like teeth set along the edges there.

But the impression remained that this was a rich game land not overcrowded with inhabitants. The Styor hunted some for sport, the lurkers for food, neither of them making big inroads on the native game. How true that was Kade learned a couple of hours later when they had made their way into the heights.

They had lingered for a breather on the top of a ridge, and ahead was a drift of mist—no, dust rising. Lik turned and two of the Ikkinni hastily moved to give him free passage.

"We stay."

"What is it?"

"One of the big herds of kwitu making the spring passage."

Kwitu, the horn-nosed creatures. But hundreds, thousands of them would have to be on the move to raise such a cloud as that. Lik sat down on a convenient ledge.

"They pass from south to north with the seasons. Sometimes it takes two days for a big herd to get through a gap." He watched the cloud of dust through narrowed eyes. "They head now for the Slit." His fingers went to his control box.

Iskug, at the other end of the line of natives gave a convulsive
jerk, his hands rising toward his collared throat, but he made
no outcry in answer to that unnecessarily brutal summons.

Kade's hand balled into a fist, until he saw Lik's sly amusement spark in his yellow, reptilian eyes. Watch out! Lik might
just double his collar pull for the pleasure of making the Terran show useless resentment. Kade's fingers relaxed, he
brushed his hand across his hide field breeches, removing a
smear of rock dust.

"There is a way into the mountains." Lik was not asking
a question of the chief hunter, he was stating a fact. Iskug had
better answer in the affirmative or suffer consequences.

"Such a one climbs high," the native's voice was husky.

"Then we climb high." Lik mimicked the Ikkinni. "And at
once." He added an unprintable emphasis, but he did not
give his guide a second collar jolt.

They did climb, from the back of the ridge, up a higher
crown, and then by a series of ledges and rough breaks to the
first slope of a mountain. The cloud of dust still hung heavy
to the east and Kade thought that now and again the wind
brought them a low mutter of sound, the bawling of the kwitu,
the clamor of countless numbers of three split hooves pounding along the same ribbon of ground.

Close to sundown the hunting party reached a plateau
where a stunted vegetation held tenaciously against the pull
of the mountain winds to afford a pocket of shelter as a spring.
Kade, kneeling beside the small pool that spring fed, was
startled when he raised his eyes to the rock surface facing him.
Carved there in deeply incised strokes into which paint had
been long ago splashed, was the life-size representation of a
kwitu, its broad nose-horned head bent until the pits which
marked the nostrils were just above the surface of the lapping
water. The unknown artist, and he had been truly an artist of
great ability, had so poised his subject that the kwitu was
visibly drinking from the lost mountain pool.

Kade sat back on his heels, held up his wrist so that he

could catch the image, as it was now suitably lighted by the setting sun, on the lens of his picture recorder. Surely this was not Styor work; the aging and erosion of the stone on which it had been carved argued a long period of time, maybe centuries, since the figure had been completed. Yet who climbed to this inaccessible place to spend hours, days, perhaps months scraping into a natural wall of stone an entirely naturalistic representation of a plains animal drinking?

"Who made that?" His usual dislike for Lik's company did not hold now. The Terran asked his question eagerly as the Overman came down to pour water over his head and shoulders.

The other regarded the drinking kwitu indifferently. "Who knows? Old, of no value."

"But the Ikkinni—"

Lik scowled. "Maybe the animals make hunt magic. This is of no value. Phaw." He pursed his lips, spat. The drop of moisture carried across, to spatter on the rump of the kwitu. Then he grinned at Kade. "No value," he repeated mockingly.

Kade shrugged. No use trying to make the Overman understand. Filling his canteen the Terran tramped back to their camp. He watched the natives, apparently not one of them noted the carving. In fact that blindness was a little too marked. Once again his fighter's sixth sense of warning stirred. Suppose that drinking beast had some symbolic religious meaning? Kade's memory provided bits of lore, that of his own race and others, Terra born and bred. Far back in the mists of forgotten time were the men of his world who had wandered as free hunters, tribesmen who had drawn on the walls of caves, painted on hides, modeled in elastic clay, the shapes of the four-footed meat they wished to slay. And then they had made powerful magic, sending the spears, the arrows, the clubs later to be used in the actual hunting, crashing against the pictures they had fashioned, believing their gods would give them in truth what they so hunted in ritual.

He would not have credited the Ikkinni with the artistic

ability to produce the carving he had just seen. But what did the off-worlders know of the free Ikkinni anyway? Their observations were based on the actions of cowered and spirit-broken slaves; on the highly prejudiced comments of masters who deemed those slaves no better than animals. Suppose that practices of that ancient hunting magic would linger on in a remote spot such as this, where perhaps no alien had ever walked? Lik had mocked such a belief in as filthy a fashion as he knew. But sometimes it was not a good thing to challenge the power inherent in things once venerated by another people. Kade had heard tales—

The Terran smiled quietly. An idea, an amusing idea was born from that point of imagination. He would have to know more of those Overman personally. Lik had mocked an old god thing. Kade began to fit one idea to another.

It was Lik himself who gave the Terran the first opening. They had eaten and were sitting by the fire, the Ikkinni banished to a suitable distance. The Overman belched, dug a finger into his mouth to rout out a shred of food eluding his tongue. Having so asserted himself, he stared at Kade.

"What matter old things to you, off-world man?" he demanded arrogantly.

"I am a trader, to a trader all things which are made with hands are of interest. There are those on other worlds who pay for such knowledge. Also . . ." he broke his answer with a calculated space of hesitation. "Such things are worth knowing for themselves."

"How so?"

"Because of the Power," Kade spoke with a seriousness gauged to impress the other.

"The Power?"

"When a man makes a thing with his hands," Kade held his own into the light of the fire, flexing his fingers slightly so that the flames were reflected from the rings which encircled the fore diget of either hand, "then something of himself enters into it. But he must shape it with his own flesh and not by the aid of a machine." A flicker of glance told him that he had Lik's full attention. The Overman was of Tadder and Tadder was one of the completely colonized worlds long held by the Styor. However, a remnant of native beliefs could still linger in a half-breed and Kade knew Tadder only too well.

"And because this thing has been made with his hands, and the idea of it first shaped in his mind, it is a part of him. If the fashioner is a man of Power and has made this work for a reason of Power, then it must follow that a portion of the Power he has tried to put into his work exists, at least for his purpose."

"This you say of those scratches on a rock?" demanded Lik incredulously, aiming a thumb at the shadows which now enveloped the spring and the carved wall behind it.

"So it might be said, if the fashioner of that carving intended it to be used as I believe he might have done." Because there was a measure of belief in Kade's own mind, his sincerity impressed the alien and the other's scoffing grin faded. "A man is a hunter and he wishes meat to fall before his spear. Therefore he makes an image of that meat, as well as he can envisage it, setting his choice of prey beside a pool where there is good water. And into this picture he puts all the Power of his mind, his heart, and his hands, centering upon his work his will that that prey come to where he had made such a carving, to fall beneath his weapon. So perhaps that happens. Wiser men than we have seen it chance so."

Lik played with his belt. His grin was quite gone. Perhaps he had a thinking mind as well as a driver's callous heartlessness. A bully was not necessarily all fool. But inducing uneasiness was a delicate and precise bit of action, Kade had no intention of spoiling this play by too much force at the start.

"It remains," he yawned, rubbed two fingers across his chin, "that there are those who have a liking for the records of such finds. And I am a trader." He returned the matter to the firm base of a commercial transaction, sure Lik would continue to think of the carving, consider its possibilities, in more than one field.

Kade succeeded so well that the next morning when he went to the pool to rinse and fill his canteen he discovered Lik standing there, studying the carving. In the brighter light of day the kwitu was less impressive, more weatherworn, but the artistry of the conception was still boldly plain.

That unknown artist had left no other trace of his passing or his living on the plateau which had survived the years. Although Kade examined every promising rock outcrop, there was not the slightest hint that anyone had crossed that expanse before their own party, though Iskug took a guide's lead with the assurance of one who knew his path.

On the far side of the plateau they descended an easy zig-zag stairway of ledges to the bottom of a canyon where the sky was a ribbon of pale silver-green far above, and their boots gritted in a coarse amber sand which identified a long-dried river bed. Their journey in the half-gloom of the depths took on an endless quality, but when they halted for cold rations at mid-day Iskug indicated a new trail, another climb toward the heights. This was the hardest pull they had so far had and the ascent brought them to another ridge.

A murmur of sound filtered up, and with the noise a haze of dust thick as fog, not yet close enough to torment throats and eyes, hanging in a murky wave about a hundred feet below. Now and then the curtain wavered and Kade could see the bobbing, dust-grayed backs of the kwitu still headed north, filling the slit below from wall to wall, the constant complaint of their bellows echoed and rechoed into a sullen roaring.

From here on their path followed ridge and ledge, gradually descending until the dust hid the road ahead. But Lik did not question Iskug, probably believing that with Lik's control of the collar, the native would not dare to lead them into danger.

They found it easy enough to thread along until they hit

the level of the dust. There Lik called a halt, stationing himself behind Iskug, his fingers on the control buttons in warning. Linked hand to hand in a line, water soaked strips of cloth tied over nose and mouth, they shuffled on, the sound of the kwitu loud enough to drown out all other noises. Now and then Kade caught a glimpse of a bull's head tossed high, heard the squall of an out of season calf, louder and more shrill than the plaint of its elders. But for the most part there was no individuality in that live ribbon.

Escape into a side pocket came before sundown. But the dull murmur of the herd continued to be heard as the hunting party made their way back into the mountains. Kade knew that the thousands of migrating kwitu would not halt because of the end of daylight. The animal trek took on awesome proportions and the Terran was duly impressed.

Iskug led them into a basin where there were trees of respectable size and the grass was as lush as on the outer plains. Before the light had quite faded, Kade noted movement to the far end of the valley and turned to Dokital, patiently waiting behind him, for an explanation.

"That is?"

"The kwitu bulls. Old. Bad. Bad here," the Ikkinni tapped his hairy forehead. "No more want female, no want clan brothers. Only want to fight. Bad."

Bulls outcast from the herd, dangerous, right enough. But Lik must have noted them too for the Overman placed the cube of a sonic in the middle of their improvised camp, setting its dial. That guardian devised by the Styor had been adjusted to those it would protect, but any newcomer would be met by sonic blast which would be wall-like in its defense of their party.

Kade awoke in the first pale suggestion of dawn, awoke to instant consciousness. And that act in itself was a warning. Under the flap of his bedroll, he drew his stunner. Then, turning his head slowly, he tried to evaluate the sound which must have alerted him.

There was a crash in the brush, followed by the enraged bellow of a kwitu bull that must have tangled with the sonic shield. Yet Kade could not accept that as what had awakened him. Something more stealthy and from a closer point— He rolled on his side as might a disturbed sleeper. Then his knees were under him and he made his feet, stunner ready.

A flick from the brush cover, and the curl of a lash caught his wrist with force enough to jerk the weapon half out of his grasp. Had Kade not been alert he might easily have been disarmed. Jerking away from that clutch, he caught his heel in the tangle of his recently quitted bag and staggered back, out of the path of sudden and certain death.

For the bellow which he had thought marked the meeting of the kwitu with the sonic protector was not that at all. A horned head thrust through a bush, small eyes red with rage and pain centered on the campsite. A horn dug turf, threw clods over humped shoulders, and a ton of mad anger on four feet plowed directly across the ashes of last night's fire toward the Terran.

Kade threw himself to the left to avoid that rush. He was enmeshed in a tangle of grass and vines and held long enough to see the kwitu stop again to paw and horn the ground. There was not an Ikkinni in sight. And Lik—where was Lik?

The chill of premonition fathered a guess. Steel had died in this wilderness. Now his successor in turn threatened. By chance, or by careful arrangement?

Kade tore his arm free of a vine, snapped a beam-shot at the kwitu. The bull had wheeled for a second charge, moving with an agility which belied its bulk. The invisible ray of force caught it across the top of the domed skull. The result was not unconsciousness for the animal, but a complete break with sanity. At a dead run the kwitu tore straight ahead.

A small tree gave under that blind attack and Kade looked as through a window at the next act of the drama.

Lik stood in the open, a queer expression of surprise and

horror distorting his handsome face. He could see the bull coming, but he made no move to avoid the headlong charge of the insane beast.

CHAPTER 4

KADE SHOUTED, swung the stunner up for a second shot at the bull. But an amazing burst of speed by the heavy animal defeated his hasty aim. The head scooped, tossed. And Lik, big as he was, arose in the air, his agonized cry shrilling above the bellow of the kwitu.

The bull whirled as the Overman hit the ground and lunged again at the feebly struggling man, its hooves tearing though the plains grass. Kade steadied on one knee, the barrel of his stunner resting on his forearm, the strength of the beam pushed to "full" as he fired.

That blast of energy must have caught the kwitu between the small eyes, and the result was the same as if an axe had cracked open its thick skull. It went to its knees, round head plowing forward so that the under jaw scrapped along the earth. Then the body struck Lik, bore him along with the impetus of that now undirected charge.

The Overman screamed once again. And his thin cry was echoed from the bushes. Out of one rusty clump an Ikkinni burst free, staggering, his hands tearing at the slave band about his throat, while the violent shaking of other bits of brush told of the agony of his fellows still governed by the control box on their injured driver.

With a groan the Ikkinni fell to his hands and knees, began to crawl painfully toward the tangle of kwitu and Overman. Kade tore at the twisted branches and vines which held him. Before he had kicked loose from that mesh the crawling native had reached the bodies, was pulling feebly at Lik.

Kade ran across the trampled ground and the Ikkinni looked up. It was Iskug, his lips drawn tight against his teeth, his eyes holding something of madness in their depths as he fought the pressure about his throat. Kade shifted the limp body of the Overman, was answered by a moan, a faint stir. The broad head of the kwitu rested on the man's middle, the weight of the heavy skull must be pressing directly on the control box.

The Terran wrestled with the bull's head, using the nose horn for a grip. At last he was able to lift it away from Lik. Blood welled from a ragged tear in the alien's thigh. Kade made an examination, using the materials from his aid pack to tend the gore. Lik might also have suffered broken bones or internal injuries, but this was his only visible wound.

Kade heard a whistling gasp of breath. Less than a foot away Iskug lay spent, a drabble of pale, pinkish blood flowing from nostrils and the corners of his now slack mouth. Beneath the down on his cheeks his naturally white skin was flushed to a purple dusk.

The Terran tightened the temporary packing on Lik's wound. The Overman was still unconscious but his breathing seemed better than Iskug's and the off-worlder sat back on his heels, making no move to touch the control box. With a laborous effort the native levered himself up. His ribs heaving as he sucked in great gasps of air. He crawled to the Overman, watching the Terran warily.

Obviously he expected opposition from Kade, but still he was going to make an effort to secure the box. What the off-worlder did then must have surprised the Ikkinni. For he moved, not to defend Lik, but to slide his arm about the hunter's shoulders, putting one hand over Iskug's to guide those hairy fingers to the belt about Lik's middle.

"Take!" he urged.

Iskug's fingers moved, fastened on that belt in a convulsive grip as a shadow struck them both. Dokital knelt on the other side of the prone Overman, went to work on the belt buckle.

As he did so Kade saw a loop of rope hanging from the native's wrist, saw, also, the patch of raw skin where too tight bonds had chafed.

"What chanced?"

Dokital pulled the loop off, flung it into the grass.

"It was tied."

"Why?"

"There was a plan. It would not aid that plan."

"A plan for a killing?"

"For a killing," Dokital agreed. "There were two plans. One different from the other."

"And one was made by this one," Kade pointed to Lik. "The other by these." The Terran nodded at the natives.

"That is so. This collar master had the saying of one plan. To kill the starwalker with a bull."

"And the other plan?"

"To let the Planner—" Dokital nodded toward the distant triple peak still visible, "decide who died."

"True spoken." Iskug's voice was a croaking whisper. He sat with the control box tight within the circle of his arm. From the bushes the rest of the hunters crawled or staggered.

Kade watched them warily. He had the stunner, a cross blast of that weapon could bring them all down before they reached him, weak as they now were.

"The Planner decided, the Spearman thrust," Dokital said. He went down on one knee again, slid Lik's knife from its sheath, his purpose very evident.

Kade deflected that blow, sending the blade home in the trampled earth a good six inches from the chest which had been the target. Red eyes smoldered as they met his.

"Will the starwalker take on a blood feud for this one?"

"It does not. But also it would know why a killing was planned."

Dokital pulled the knife from the ground, ran his finger along the clean sweep of the blade. Then from that length of perma-steel he looked to Iskug.

"It has said that these two are not as one," the native from the post remarked.

Iskug fondled the control box. "Let the starwalker break this thing so it and it and it," he pointed to his men, "no longer must crawl at a lifted finger, but may once again walk straight in the sun as warriors."

Regretfully Kade shook his head. To meddle with the intricate control box might mean death for all those so tragically linked with that diabolical thing. He said as much, trying to to make it clear.

"This still lives." He stooped to adjust the bandage about Lik's thigh. "It may have an answer to the box."

"Not to go back!" Iskug cried, was echoed by an affirmative chorus from the hunters.

Dokital fingered his own collar. The capture of this control meant no freedom for him. But he did not question Iskug's decision.

Kade asked another question as the Overman moaned.

"And for these?" He pointed to Lik, himself, Dokital.

Iskug hesitated. It was plain that at least two of the three offered a problem for which he had no quick solution. Yet it was also apparent he had no ill will for either Kade or the post native.

"For this," he turned almost with relief to Lik and drew his finger down his chest in a motion which needed no clearer translation.

"Not so. Perhaps it can break the magic of the collar," Kade countered. "The kill was mine," he slapped one hand on the dusty head of the kwitu. "It is mine," he nodded at the Overman whose life he had saved, at least for a space, by that same lucky shot. Whether such reasoning would hold with the Ikkinni he had yet to learn.

Dokital struck in. "It is now slave to the starwalker, taken as in a net."

The justice of that appeared to appeal to Iskug.

"It is broken," he observed without any concern. "So it can not serve."

"But it can talk, as the starwalker has said. Now come wet winds." Dokital gestured at the mountains about them. "We must have fire, cover."

There were clouds massing about the peaks, a fog creeping down to blot out the heights. Even Kade, knowing little of Klorian weather, saw there was a change for the worse in the making. Iskug studied Lik. With very obvious reluctance he gave orders for a litter to be fashioned out of the alien's sleeping bag and saplings from the grove. Hoping that the Overman could survive the handling, Kade got the inert body on the litter with Dokital's aid, and together they were left to carry on at the end of the procession heading for the nearest mountain wall.

By the time the rock escarpment was just before them the hesitant sunshine of the morning had gone and a murk close to twilight settled in. Iskug appeared to have some goal in view. He turned northwest at the edge of the slope and his pace became a trot Kade and Dokital, the litter between them, could not equal. As they lagged behind the Ikkinni dropped back, his impatience plain, to order the hunters to help at the litter poles.

Kade trotted beside Lik. He was sure that he had seen the Overman's eyes open and close again quickly, and he had not missed the movement of the hand groping for the control no longer there. Lik was not only conscious again, but enough in command of his faculties to want to assume leadership of his slaves once more. Yet now he lay once more with closed eyes, the more dangerous for that ability in his present condition to act a role.

The litter bearers passed between two pillars of rock and Kade dropped back. Then the storm broke in great pelting drops of rain, stinging as might pellets of ice against their skins. With a burst of speed they came into the shelter Iskug had sought where an overhand of rock shielded a hollow in the mountain side. The place was not a cave but the roof arched well over their heads and kept out a good measure of the rain.

Kade watched Iskug dig into the gravel at the rear of the hollow, bringing out of hiding an armload of the greasy, long-burning river reed stalks which were the best fire material on Klor. Since there was no reed-bearing river within miles as far as the Terran knew, such a cache meant that there must often be occupation of this shelter.

His own problem was Lik. The Ikkinni had set the litter well to the back of the half cave and left its occupant strictly alone. Iskug still hugged the control box to himself, having rigged it in an improvised belt of trap net against his middle. As far as Kade could see there was no chance of the injured Overman regaining his power. But he was also certain that Lik would try just that. Now the Terran squatted down beside the litter, ostensibly to inspect the other's bandages.

There came a crack of light and sound mingled, slashing down just outside the overhang. Kade started. Then his hand swept around to strike at the wrist above those fingers closing on his stunner. His gaze met that of the alien on the litter with a grim warning.

"Do not try that now."

Knowing that Lik would never accept him as an ally after this small defeat, Kade counterattacked swiftly, hoping to surprise some morsel of information out of the other.

"I am not meat for your killing, Overman!"

Lik's hatred was plain, and now nakedly open in the glare of his yellow eyes. The lips, feline flat against his teeth, were in a snarl of rage. Kade pushed his point.

"Why? Because I am Terran, or because I am I?" He could conceive of no reason for a personal feud between them, though he had disliked the other from their first meeting. Perhaps that instinctive revulsion had been mutual, and carried to an extreme by the alien's temperament.

Lik did not answer. His hands now lay clenched upon his

41

middle where once they had played over the keys of the control and he closed his eyes, his whole body expressing his stubborn refusal to reply.

Iskug's fire blazed, driving out a portion of the damp storm chill with welcome heat. As the hunters gathered about it, their leader placed the control box between his knees, turning it this way and that in the light of the flames. Once he raised it in his two hands as if to cast it into the heart of the fire and from behind Kade heard Lik's small, evil chuckle.

Spurred by that sound the Terran shouted, "No!" Ikkinni heads turned. He added swiftly, "The Overman wishes that!"

Iskug stood up, tucked the control box back in his net sling, came to stand over Lik. Kade saw the alien did not flinch even when a spear pricked his flesh at heart level.

"Strike, dirt eater," Lik's lips shaped a grimace which might have been meant for a smile. "Strike and then guard that box, for it will bind every one of you!"

One of the other hunters came hurrying across, loomed over the wounded alien.

"Make that not so!" He ordered.

Again Lik laughed. "It could not if it would," he retorted, spirit undiminished. "The secret is not its—"

"It may be right," Kade pointed out. This is a Styor thing. And Lik is not Styor."

The Overman's reaction to that was unexpected. Kade might have struck purposefully at a half-healed wound, bringing again agonizing pain. Lik jerked up on the litter, his fist striking the Terran on the shoulder, knocking Kade off balance so that he sprawled back. Again those fingers snatched at his holstered weapon, and this time the off-worlder was too late to prevent loss. But he was leaping again for Lik as the alien snapped the beam button. There was no visible answer to that half aimed shot. And a moment later Kade's hold was on the other's wrist, twisting.

As suddenly as he had attacked the other, Lik surrendered,

panting under the Terran's weight. And Kade had freedom to see what the stunner had done.

Iskug rolled on the gravel, his face again dusky, his hands tearing at the collar. Beyond him the rest of his fellows were down in the same torture. Then the head tracker gasped, half leaped, to fall back, but he was still breathing. The hands at his throat tugged again at the collar. And under that grip, feeble as it must have been, the band of silvery stuff broke.

He dropped the broken circlet, rubbed his throat with his fingers. Two of the other hunters lay still, one with his knees drawn up to his chest in a silent expression of his death pain. But the others moved sluggishly, almost as if they could not believe they were still living. Each, witnessing Iskug's luck, put hands to their own collars, snapped the bands easily.

Iskug cradled the control box between his hands once again. Cautiously he raised the cube to the level of his ear, shook it with increasing vigor. Then, in his fingers, the thing came apart, showered a rain of crumbled container and small, unidentifiable interior parts. Kade began to deduct what had happened.

Lik had struck that control with the beam from the Terran stunner. And that force thrust had reacted violently upon the Styor mechanism, not only deadening the collars—after one intense, final attack on their wearers—but ending by burning out completely the whole installation. In that same instant that the off-worlder realized the possibilities of the weapon now in his hand, Lik must have followed the same line of reasoning. For the alien lost his head.

He heaved under Kade's hold, fingers gouging and tearing at the Terran's eyes, his teeth snapping as might an animal's on the flesh of the other's forearm. And such was the wild passion of that attack that, for a second, Kade was forced on the defensive. Lik was pounds heavier than his opponent, and much of that poundage was well-developed muscle. Unlike Buk at the post, this Overman had not followed the slothful existence of the usual slave driver. Rather, his hunting expeditions had kept him in good physical condition.

Now, because he had lost all desire for self-preservation, he was intent only on destroying Kade, Kade's knowledge, Kade's suddenly vital weapon. Lik was as dangerous as the kwitu bull. And the Terran sensed that he was now fighting for his life.

He broke Lik's hold on his throat when by lucky chance he drove his knee down upon the other's wound. With a yelp, the Overman twisted, relaxing steel-tight fingers for a moment. Kade brought into play the scientifically taught infighting, part of the Service's training. He made connections with the other's square jaw at just the right angle, rolling away as a spear flashed over his hunched shoulder bit deep enough to send the answering spout of blood up on the breast of his own tunic.

"Why?"

But there was no reason really to ask why Iskug had killed. The Ikkinni was exacting payment for all the months, perhaps years, that he had lived under Lik's control. Now that the box was dead and he no longer needed Lik's knowledge of it, the Overman ceased to exist. But he took with him into the dark the answer to Kade's own questions. Why had the Terran been set up for the kill, and by whose orders?

In return they had the reply to the Styor's dominance on Klor. A drastic remedy though. Two out of seven died to achieve freedom—too high a price. Or did the Ikkinni think that way? Kade found an extra undershirt in his bedroll, collected every bit of the disintegrated control box from the gravel, adding to that the remains of one of the collars, which also crumbled at his touch. The Ikkinni watched him, still massaging their throats. Dokital, his collar conspicuous in that company now, joined the Terran in his task, his long fingers shifting out bits of wire, small wheels, a fragment of what might have been a charge disc.

"This is broken," he commented.

"There are those who perhaps can understand even a broken thing."

"Those in the stars?"

Kade nodded, knotted his improvised bag carefully. "If such is understood, next time there may be no more who die."

"A next time there?" Dokital's eyes were alive, brilliant flames of awakened fire.

"A next time, when we know more, yes." Kade promised.

"The starwalker returns to its kind?" Iskug broke in.

"It returns to the fire of its kind," Kade spoke firmly. He hoped the newly liberated men would not try to hold him prisoner.

"It returns, then hunters come—they who hunt men." Iskug looked stubborn.

"Not so," Kade objected. "It will have a story."

"What story?"

"That there was trouble with the kwitu and much killing by horn and hoof. This is the time of the great trek to the north and there is the storm. The kwitu were maddened by the storm, they came upon the camp where the sonic did not work. All died save it, and it." He pointed to Dokital and himself. "It and it were sleeping apart. And those who have planned for some deaths will be told of others come by ill chance. Who shall say this is not true?"

Iskug considered that. For the first time he smiled, thinly.

"The tale is good for it is mixed truth and careful thought. Who not in the mountains can prove the forked words are not straight? The collar master meant death for the starwalker, so arranged that we leave camp, that the sonic was silent. Then came the death, but not as it was planned. Yes, those," he spat, made a sign of vileness with two fingers, "could believe. And who seeks the dead to wear slave rings? The trail is open." He reversed his spear, driving it head down in the gravel.

"It says this also," he continued. "Discover what that

45

weapon from the stars can do, and then give life to more slave ones. It lays this on you as a fire oath."

"So shall it be, as Iskug says," Kade agreed. He had gained his point, now he was eager to return to the post where he could start to work the affair of stunner against Styor control.

CHAPTER 5

"BUT WHY WAS THE SONIC OFF?" Santoz leaned across the mess table to ask almost querulously. "Those Overmen know their drill out in the backs. Why, the camp could have been overrun by lurkers."

"Yes, why did the sonic fail?" But when Abu echoed that he was not asking a question of the defensive Kade, rather of the whole Terran Team. "Did you examine it afterwards, ascertain whether it failed through any mechanical defect?"

"You can't tell anything about a machine crushed by an angry kwitu bull," Kade pointed out, treading this conversational trail as warily as he might have lurked on the fringe of a hostile camp. He had had three days during his march back to the post with Dokital to prune and polish his story, working up bits of collaborative detail with the Ikkinni. And he hoped they both had the proper answers for any question which would come from either Styor or Terran.

"Very true," Abu agreed. "And you were asleep when the invasion of the camp occurred."

"Yes." So far he had woven truth into later fiction.

Che'in voiced a faint giggle. "Almost one could imagine," he drawled, "that our young Teammate here was in the greatest danger of all at that moment. How fortuitous, Whitehawk, that you should have awakened in good time. The Spirits of Outer Space would seem to favor you. Also, of course, Whitehawk could not determine, even if he had had it for inspection, whether the sonic was functioning properly. Those are a product of the Styor and so another of the small mysteries which so tantalizingly spice a Trader's life." He lapsed into silence, still smiling, a smile which urged them all to enjoy a subtle joke unnecessary to put into crass speech.

"The sonic's failure had been reported to Cor," Abu remarked in the tone of one making an official statement.

"Yes, it might almost seem that someone paid a high price for a bad bargain." Kade tried to needle some response from these three who certainly possessed more knowledge of Klorian affairs.

Santoz looked baffled, Che'in amused. The reply was left to their commanding officer.

"We will not go into that." The Commander's retort had the snap of an order. "The High-Lord-Pac will conduct the investigation. It is out of our hands, since the dead and missing are not post personnel."

Proper investigation for which side, Kade wanted to ask and knew that would be fruitless. He got up.

"That is exactly what happened." He caught a measuring glance from Abu, and was no longer so sure of himself.

"The report has gone to Cor. Undoubtedly we shall hear more."

Again Che'in giggled. "When one digs too deeply into the bottom of a still pond, one stirs up a quantity of mud," he observed. "And the High-Lord-Pac is not one to dirty his gloves of justice. Stalemate, commander?"

"We may be glad for that. You," Abu regarded Kade straightly, this time with a critical and unsympathetic eye. "Walk softly, my friend. You will take over the com transmitter. I have a wish for you to be at hand if your testimony should suddenly be needed."

To tend the transmitter, in a station where off-world messages were few, might have meant a period of unrelieved boredom. But Kade brought with him the tape which had been Steel's record, and sitting where he could see the alarm light

47

above the relay board, plugged in an ear-reader to hear the words of a man who had been killed somewhere on Klor—just as he might have been killed four days ago.

The expressionless words which spun long sentences of trade detail, descriptions of the country and the natives into his ears were monotonous, and he had to guess what should have been in the gaps. This tape had not been edited for a stranger's use, a man's record was for his own advantage, a reminder of details pertinent to his particular post job. Kade had not expected a concise listing, just a leading hint or two.

He judged by the abundance of notes on flora and fauna that Steel had had a keen interest in the biology of the planet, narrowing eventually to observations concerning the plains vegetation, the kwitu herds, and the mountain valleys.

When those two unusual words were mentioned, Kade did not at first realize their significance. Then he straightened, his swift movement jerking loose the reader cord. Had he really heard that? The Terran thumped the small plug back into his ear, waited tensely for a repeat of that unbelievable phrase. Unbelievable because it had been uttered in another tongue, one perhaps twenty men in the Service, and those men scattered on like number of planets, could have translated.

"Peji equals sunkakan!"

So he had been right! Those two words in Lakota Sioux had cropped up in the middle of a description of a mountain valley Steel had surveyed, planted there perhaps to conceal their importance from any future user of the tape, save one of his own tribe. But had Steel then been expecting trouble, or personal danger? And how could the other have forseen he would be replaced on Klor by a fellow tribesman. No, Steel must have used that phrase because the words themselves had a strong meaning for him, a meaning connected with his own racial past.

Peji, grass, the grass of the North American plains where Sioux warriors had ruled. *Sunkakan*: horses, the horses which the white man had brought, but which turned drifting primitive hunters into the finest irregular cavalry his home world had ever seen, aided them to hold back an encroaching mechanical civilization for a surprising number of years. Hold back conquerors! Kade pulled the plug from his ear, stared at the com board without seeing one of its buttons or levers.

That was history, and history was repetitious. The Amerindian, mounted, had held back the American Frontiersman, for a time. But earlier he had done something else. He had driven back, almost annihilated an older culture, based on domination and slavery. The Commanche, the Apache, the Navajo, mounted, had pushed their would-be Spanish rulers out of the Southwest, spoiled, removed from the earth the haciendas spreading northward, the mission-held lands, liberating the slave-peons either by death or by adoption into their own savage ranks. The Spanish, secure with their superior weapons, their horses, had crept up into the deserts and plains. The Indians had seen, had taken mounts from the Spanish corrals, had come raiding so that in less than a century, perhaps a half-century, the Spanish wave northward had broken, washed back, been put on the defensive even in the strongholds of Mexico.

The horse put by chance and blindness into the hands of born horsemen!

Had that been Steel's dream too? Feverishly Kade went back to his listening, ran through the whole tape. He was sure now he could pick out hints, that something of that idea had been in the dead man's mind. But only that one phrase was clear. Introduce horses into a horseless world, a world of plains where the grass would sustain the breed. Put the horse into the hands of natives now immured in the mountains. Make of them lightning raiders who could hit and run, darting back into mountain hideouts where the airborne reprisals of the Styor could not follow. A band of attackers who could split into individual riders only to regroup when the danger of pursuit was past, and how could an air patrol cover the scattering of half a troop of men all riding in different directions? Just as the outlying haciendas of the Spanish had fallen one after another to whittling raids, enemies striking without warning out of the plains, so could the lords of Klor, in their widely separated holdings, be victimized by raiders who had at their command a method of swift transportation which was not a machine to be serviced or to lack fuel, which would reproduce itself without any need for technologists or factories.

Kade's enthusiasm grew as his imagination painted a host of details. He believed he saw a way in which the High-Lord-Pac could be used to initiate the Styor downfall. A selection of tri-dees of horses, shown to an alien already enough interested in off-world animals to pay the fantastic fee for the importation of a bear, ought to do the trick.

Kade faced a new thought. To get horses here to Klor might be easy. But horses for the Ikkinni—What proof had he that the native hunters of Klor would take as readily to the use of alien animals as his ancestors had done? Suppose the Ikkinni were neither natural born riders, nor could be made into passable horsemen? And they had no history of domesticated animals, even the dogs and cats which had accompanied his own Terran kind for so long were not to be found on Klor.

Yet Dokital had been fascinated by the bear, had asked about the relationship between it and the Terran. He could try some propaganda on the one Ikkinni with whom he had a tenuous bond approaching friendship.

Since their return from the hunt Kade had avoided the native mainly for Dokital's protection, since Buk, aroused by the death of his co-worker, had thrown off his lethargy and was now playing the slave driver with a harshness Abu did not challenge. Kade sensed that any special notice of the young Ikkinni now would bring him to the unfavorable attention of the Overman.

When at last Santoz came to spell him at the coms, he answered the other's small talk absently, eager to get to his room. But as he crossed the courtyard he caught a glimpse of faint light in a window slit which should be totally dark. And he threw back the door panel, to confront an Ikkinni, hairy back toward him, on his hands and knees beside the wall bunk, striving to open the storage place in its base.

Kade stood still, his fingers flexed not too far from the butt of his stunner. Then, without turning his head, the other spoke.

"It has been waiting."

"And searching. For what?"

"For that which was brought from the mountains." Dokital arose. As all the post slaves he was unarmed, spears issued only for hunting trips. Kade did not believe the other would attack against a stunner or attract a swift vengeance from Buk, but his attitude was far from friendly.

"And what does it want with the remains of the slave box?" Kade came into the room, shut the door panel.

"Buk wears a box also." Now Dokital turned, faced Kade, his shoulders slightly hunched, the look of an untamed thing about him, ready to offer battle if he could get what he wanted. "The starwalker can break the box of Buk, he has not done so. Nor has he given the box which was broken to others." The hostility was now in the open.

"Does it forget what happened when the box of Lik was broken," Kade kept his voice low, fearing that even a murmur might carry beyond the walls. Let a hint of what he had hidden reach Abu and he would be bundled off planet, his career ruined, perhaps a labor gang sentence waiting. And let that same rumor, even distorted, carry to the Styor and it could mean the death of every Trader on Klor, the banishment certainly of the only weapon the rulers allowed the Terrans to handle. "Some died because the box was broken," he tried to impress the native. "Let Buk's box feel this," he tapped the holstered stunner," and maybe Dokital will be it who this time loses breath."

But the Ikkinni appeared unmoved by that argument. "Better it dies and some live." He held up his fingers and then deliberately folded those of one hand under. "Let this be so, starwalker. Yet still are these free." He wriggled the raised ones vigorously. "To lose breath is better than to run back and forth while Buks says 'do this, do that.'"

"Dokital says so, but will the others here agree?" Kade pointed to the fist of closed fingers. "Has it spoken to them concerning the broken box?"

"Had it spoken," Dokital answered with a deliberate spacing of words which gave a weight beyond their simplicity, "the starwalker might have lost breath—all the starwalkers —so that what they carry could lie here," he slapped the fingers of one hand across the palm of the other. "It waited but the starwalker had not broken Buk's box. Now it will talk, and things shall be done."

Kade slammed the full weight of his body against the Ikkinni, bore the native back to the bunk and held him there in spite of his struggles.

"Listen!" He almost spat into the rage-darkened face inches away from his own. "Buk will be taken at the right time. Move now and the Styor will blast us all into nothingness. Let me find out how the box is broken and perhaps we can move without men dying."

"Time! There is no time left, starwalker. A message comes from Cor. The starwalker is to go to the collar masters. When they discover what has happened it will lose breath and no starwalker can save—"

A message from the Styor city. But he had heard nothing of that. The Ikkinni might have read the Terran's puzzlement in the slight slacking of his hold.

"It speaks the truth!" Dokital's body arched under his in a last frantic attempt to gain freedom. Then they both froze at a sound from without, a rap on the door panel.

Kade loosed his hold on the native, pulled away from the

bunk, edged to the door, his stunner out and centered at a point between Dokital's red eyes.

"Who is there?" he called over his shoulder.

"Buk."

Dokital, still sprawled on the bunk, tensed, his head turning from right to left as if he searched for sight of a weapon he had no hope in finding. Kade gestured imperatively. The Ikkinni slipped to the floor, opened the base storage space and pulled himself into hiding.

The Terran took his time about freeing the thumb lock on the corridor door, waiting to see that space closed. Dokital would have to double up painfully in such a small cranny, but discomfort was better than having Buk discover him here.

To Kade's surprise, the Overman, hesitating on the threshold, made no attempt to look about the room. If he had come hunting a missing slave he did not disclose that fact. Instead his attitude was uneasy and Kade's confidence grew.

"The Overman wishes?" the Terran demanded with chill crispness.

"Information, starwalker," Buk blurted out with little of his usual assumption of equality with the Traders. He slid one booted foot into the room and Kade guessed that he did not want to state his business in the open. The Terran stood aside and Buk oozed in, shut the door panel and set his plump shoulders against it as if to stave off some threatened invasion.

"There is a story," he began, looking none too happy. "Now there are those who say that Lik saw a certain thing by the water and mocked that thing openly, then he was slain by that which he mocked."

Kade leaned back against the end of the bunk. "There was an old, old carving on a rock by the pool," he spoke gravely, "which Lik spat upon and mocked, yes. Then with the next dawn the kwitu which was like unto that pictured by the pool, came and rent him. This is no story, for with my two eyes I saw it."

"And the thing by the pool. Who made it so?" Buk persisted.

"Who live in the mountains, Overman?"

Buk's tongue, thick and a brownish red, moistened his blubbery lips. His fat rolls of fingers played a tattoo on either side of the control box at the fore of his ornate belt. His uneasiness was so poorly concealed that Kade's half plan, shelved at Lik's death, came to life again. Now he decided upon a few embellishments. If Buk was superstitious the Terran could well add to his growing fears.

"I have been asking myself," Kade said, as if he were musing aloud and not addressing Buk, "why it was that the kwitu did not turn horn and hoof on me, for I was easy meat when the sonic failed us. However the hunt was not for me, but for Lik, and he was not the nearest nor the first that the bull sighted. It is true I had not mocked that which was carved beside the pool, rather did I speak well of it, since such old things are revered among *my* people."

"But to believe so is the foolishness of lesser creatures," Buk's tongue made its nervous lip journey a second time. "Such thinking is not for masters."

"Perhaps so," Kade made polite but plainly false agreement to that sentiment. "Yet among the stars many things come to pass which no man can explain, or has not found a proper explanation to fit the circumstances. All I know is that I breathe and walk, and Lik does not, where Lik mocked and I did not. Perhaps this adds to something of meaning, perhaps not. But while I am on Klor I shall be careful not to mock what I do not understand."

"Foolishness!" Buk grinned sickly. "The collared ones can not slay with a picture!"

"Not they, perhaps. But I have heard also of a Planner, a Netter, and a Spearman."

Buk laughed again, but this time there was no mirth in that sound, it was close to the snarl of a rat cornered and knowing fear.

"Rocks! Mountains!" he jeered.

Kade shrugged. "I have told you what I know, Overman. Is this what you would have of me?"

Buk fumbled with the door panel, stepped back into the courtyard corridor, still facing the Terran almost as if he feared turning his back upon the off-worlder. He muttered something and was gone, slouching, his bristly head sunk a little between his shoulders.

Kade slammed shut the panel as Dokital crawled out of his hiding place. For a long moment they eyed each other, but the will to struggle was gone. The Ikkinni whipped out of Kade's room, heading in the opposite direction to the one Buk had taken.

The Terran turned back to his tapes. Since the High-Lord-Pac had purchased the bear for collection there must exist some tri-dee from which the Styor had made his selection. And among them might just be one of a horse. Equines had been exported to a score of Terran colonized planets and should be listed on the Trade tapes.

Only a small portion of his mind was occupied by that search. Dokital's demand for action, Buk's display of superstitious fear, the attempt to murder him by the sonic failure; a hint there, a half-disclosed fact elsewhere— Kade had the breathless sensation of one confronted by a complicated tangle and ordered to have it unraveled within an impossibly short time.

How limited that time might be he learned only a few moments later. Commander Abu came across the courtyard with the news.

"They are sending a hop-ship from Cor to pick up the bear," he announced. "And since the High-Lord-Pac has asked for a report on the hunt trouble, you might as well go along with the transport. Here," he held a box of tri-dees. "We'll suggest to his lordship that, because of the trouble, the Service will be glad to offer him his choice of any of these items. But don't be too blatant. The Styor want their bribes shoved in their pockets around some corner when no one is looking, rather than slapped into an outheld hand."

"You are going, too?"

The other nodded. "Pomp and ceremony," he said wearily. "Commander speaks to planet governer. Oh, check your stunner in before you leave. No one wears an off-world weapon in Cor."

As Kade hurriedly packed his jump bag he had no time to check the box of tri-dees. Nor did he see Dokital when he went to leave his stunner.

When the Terrans reached the landing apron Kade stood aside to allow Abu to proceed him up the ship's ramp. And, as the younger man set foot on that slender link between ship and ground he experienced a sudden sharp pull at his scalp lock. Kade's trained body went into action, falling back at the pull, but not quickly enough to carry his attacker with him. The grip was released and he sprawled clumsily on his back. As he scrambled up he looked around.

There was nothing to be seen, his assailant had vanished. He examined his small twist of hair with his fingers. The tight braid worn by his people was intact, and he could guess no reason for that odd assault at the foot of the Styor ship.

CHAPTER 6

COR AROSE ABRUPTLY from the rolling Klorian plain with insolent refusal to accommodate alien architecture to a frontier world. The city might have been lifted entirely from some other Styor-controlled planet and set down here bodily with all its conical towers, their glitter-tipped spearlike crests pointed into the jade sky. Arrogantly, they were not a part of the ochre landscape on which their foundations rested.

Since Styor ships were not adapted to Terran physique

Kade had spent most of the trip trying to control a rebellious stomach and screaming nerves. Now he cultivated as impassive a set of features as he could while waiting on the landing strip for the arrival of the bear cage.

Gangs of Ikkinni slaves were at labor, with Overman half-breeds from half a dozen different Styor-controlled worlds in command. But the lords themselves were not to be seen. The pilot of the ship which had brought the Traders must be of the pure blood, none other ever being given a post of authority. And the Portmaster, invisible in his vantage chamber somewhere in the heights above them, would be Styor.

Kade, seeing no official greeters, knew again the prick of anger at this deliberate down grading of the Traders. The omission of such civilities was more pointed when a slender private-flyer set down half the field away from the freighter and an almost instaneous swirl of activity there marked deference paid to some outplains lordling. The Terran took tight grip on his temper, promising himself that this time nothing he saw in the Styor stronghold, no insult covert and subtle, or open and complete, would provoke him into answer. The only trouble was, as he knew very well, Kade Whitehawk was not and never would be a proper exponent of the Policy.

Styor traveled in carrying-chairs. Overmen were on platforms, borne by slaves. Terran Traders walked along the canyon-deep avenues of Cor. The polished surface of tower walls flashed, dazzling to off-world eyes. There were no windows to break their lower stories, simply an oval door recessed slightly, always firmly closed, to be sighted here and there. Not a scrap of vegetation grew anywhere about the bases of those towers. But when Kade tilted his head to look up, he could sight indentations masked in green-blue, in green-green, in yellow-green, marking sky-rooted gardens of exotics from the stars.

A protesting whimper from the cage slung between transport poles made known that the bear had again recovered from the journey drug. The Terran jogged forward to speak soothingly. He must not allow the animal to become so thoroughly frightened as to make a bad impression when it met its new owner for the first time, especially not when Kade's purpose was to urge that owner to consider more such imports.

In spite of his discomfort on board the transport he had examined the contents of the sample box and was happily aware of the presence therein of a certain tri-dee print. He hooked that box to his belt, carrying nothing in his hands. At least in that he perserved a small measure of difference between Terran and burdened slave.

The heart of Cor was the Pac Tower. More than one garden feathered its length and the Terrans, together with the bear, found themselves in the highest of those where the foliage was almost that of their earth. The strips of sod which formed its paths could hardly be distinguished from the green grass of their mother world.

Released by Kade, the bear stood in the middle of a small clearing, head up, sniffing. Then, its attention caught by the laden branches of a berry bush, it shuffled purposefully for that lure.

"This is the new one?"

There was no mistaking the slurred voice of a Styor. Into the simplest sentence, Kade thought, the older masters of the star lanes could pack an overabundent measure of arrogance, as well as the ever present underwash of ennui. The Terran turned to face one of the floating chairs, hovering a foot or two above the shaved turf, bearing on its cushioned seat a Styor of unmistakably high rank.

The jeweled, scaled mask of an adult male hid half of the face, and the headdress above that, as well as the noble's robe, was ostentatiously plain. Only the great gemmed thumb ring, covering that diget from base to nail, signified the exaulted status of its wearer.

"As was promised, lord," Abu replied.

The chair floated on and the bear, hunched down to comb

berries into a gaping mouth, looked up. For a long moment the animal from Terra regarded the chair, and perhaps the man in it, appraisingly. Kade was ready for trouble. He knew that the bear must have been conditioned at the breeding farm for all eventualities which its first owners could foresee in an alien home. But reactions to the unusual could not always be completely prepared for, or against.

Apparently floating chairs, and Styor lords in them, had been a part of the bear's training. It grunted, unimpressed, and then turned back to the more important occupation of testing these new and interesting fruits.

"This is acceptable," the Styor lord conceded. "Let those who have such duties be informed as to the care." The chair made a turn and then stopped dead. The occupant might have been suddenly reminded of another matter.

"There was a report brought to Pac attention."

Kade discovered that an utterly emotionless tone could rasp like a threat.

"A report was made" Abu agreed.

"Follow. Pac will hear."

The chair swept on at a speed which brought the Terrans to a trot. They passed under the arch of an open door, crossed the anteroom of the garden, and came into a bare chamber with a dias at one end, to which the Styor's chair sped, setting down with precision in the exact middle of that platform. And that landing was a signal which brought from two doors flanking the dias, Styor guards, to draw up in a brilliant pea-cocking of jewels, inlaid ceremonial armor and off-world weapons, between the Terrans and the High-Lord-Pac.

"There was a slaying in the mountains," the ruler of Klor observed, seemingly having no attention for either of the off-worlders before him, his stare fixed upon empty space a good yard or so above their heads.

"That is so, lord," Abu agreed with equal detachment.

"The saying is that a sonic failed."

"That is so, lord," echoed the Terran Commander, adding nothing to the formal words.

Kade, studying the half-masked faces of the Styors before him, especially that of the High-Lord-Pac, experienced anew the distaste which had always been a part of the old, old Terran distrust for the reptilian. Those visors, sharply pointed in a snout-like excrescence above the nose, imparted a lizard look to all Styor. And in the person of the High-Lord-Pac that quality was oddly intensified until one could almost believe that there *was* no humanoid countenance behind the scaled material.

"When the sonic failed, an Overman and some of his hunters were killed by kwitu," the High-Lord-Pac continued in flat exposition. "And after his death several of the collared ones fled to the mountains, his control over them being destroyed."

"The truth is as the great one says."

"The starwalker who was with these hunters, he swears to this?"

"He stands before the great one now. Let the asking be made so that he may reply with his own mouth."

That lizard's snout descended a fraction of an inch. Kade could not be certain whether the eyes behind those gem-bordered slits saw him even now.

"Let him speak concerning this happening."

Kade, striving to keep his voice as precise and cold as the Commander's, retold his story—his edited story. Faced only by that array of masks he had no hint as to whether or not they believed him. And when he had done, the comment upon his version of the disaster came obliquely.

"Let this be done," intoned the noble on the dias. "That all sonics be checked before they are issued for use. Also let the master-tech answer to Pac concerning this matter. The audience is finished."

The chair arose, moved straight ahead as the honor guard hurriedly snapped to right and left offering free passage. Kade had barely time to dodge aside as the Styor ruler passed. Was this all? Would they have no further meeting and a chance to offer the High-Lord-Pac more off-world curiosities?

An Overman guided the Terrans to a room not far above street level, close to the slave quarters. Kade waited for enlightenment as his superior officer crossed the chamber, dropped his jumpbag on a seat which was no more than a hard bench jutting out of the wall. A roll of woven mats piled at one end suggested that this also must serve as a bed when the need arose.

"What now?" Kade finally asked.

"We wait. Sometime the High-Lord-Pac will be in the mood for amusement or enlightenment. Then we shall be summoned. Since we do not exist except to supply his whims, such a time may come within the hour, tomorrow or next week."

Certainly not a very promising forecast, Kade decided. He opened the tri-dee holder and, kneeling on the floor, he set its contents out upon the bench, sorting the beautifully colored small slides. There were so lifelike that one longed to reach into the microcosm and touch the frozen figures into life and movement.

Here were the smaller, long domesticated animals, cats, dogs, exotic fowl, a curved-horned goat, a bovine family of bull, cow and calf. Then came the wild ones—or the species which had once been wild—felines, represented by lion, tiger, black leopard; a white wolf, deer. Kade discarded a bear slide, and eliminated the elephants and the rest of the larger wild kind which could not be shipped this far out into space. Then he took out the last slide of all, balanced it on his palm, examining it avidly. To his eyes it was irresistible. But how would the High-Lord-Pac see it.

Abu had no present interest in the display of trade goods and his continued silence finally drew his companion's attention. The Terran Team Commander got up from the bench, stood now by the door through which they had entered. There were no windows here. A subdued light, dim to their off-world senses, came from a thin rod running completely around the room where ceiling joined wall. But that light was not so dim as to disguise Abu's attitude. He was waiting, or listening, or expecting—

Kade arose, still holding his choice of tri-dees. They were without weapons in the heart of the undeclared enemy's territory. And Abu's stance brought that fact home to the younger man. When the Commander spoke he hardly more than shaped the words with his lips, using the tongue of their own world rather than Trade talk.

"Someone is coming. Walking."

Not a Styor visitor then, unless a guard on duty. A second later the eyepatch in the door panel glowed. Abu waited for a moment, and then acknowledged with a slap from his open palm directly below the small screen. The light flashed off, they viewed a foreshortened snap of an Overman. Abu slapped a second time, granting admittance.

"Hakam Toph," the stranger announced himself. "First Keeper of off-world animals."

Abu made the same formal introduction in return, naming himself and then Kade.

Toph showed more interest in Kade.

"It is the one who cares for beasts?"

Abu sat down on the bench, leaving the answering to Kade.

"It is," he replied shortly. The Overman was using the speech of an Ikkinni driver, and that in itself was an insult to the Traders.

"This one would know the habits of the new beast."

"A record tape was sent," Kade pointed out. He held up his hand at eye level, apparently more absorbed in the tri-dee he had selected from his samples, than in a sale already made.

And the Overman, catching sight of the array of plates on the shelf, came on into the room eagerly, drawn to the strange exhibits to be seen. Kade, nursing that last tri-dee stepped aside, allowing Toph to finger the small vivid scenes of beasts in their natural setting. The Overman was plainly excited at such a wealth. But at last he began to glance at the plate Kade still held, while firing a series of questions concerning the rest. When the Terran did not put his plate down or mention it, Toph came directly to the point.

"That is also an off-world beast?"

"That is so." But still Kade did not offer him the plate.

"That is one which is rare?"

"One," replied Kade deliberately, "which on our world is and has long been prized highly. It belongs to warriors who ride, by our customs, not borne on the shoulders of men or in chairs of state but on the backs of these beasts. Even into battle do they so ride. And among us the warriors who so ride are held in honor."

"Ride on the back of a beast!" Toph looked prepared to challenge such an outrageous statement. "It would see!" He held out his hand in demand and Kade allowed him to take the plate.

"So." Toph expelled breath in a hiss which might have signified either admiration or contempt. "And warriors ride upon this beast for honor?"

"That is so."

"You have seen them?"

Kade plunged. "On my world I am of a warrior people. I have ridden so behind those who are my overlords."

Toph glanced from the Terran back to the tri-dee plate.

"These beasts could live on Klor?"

"On Klor, yes; in Cor, no." Kade proceeded with the caution of a scout on the war trail, fearing to push too much or too fast.

"Why so?"

"Because they graze the grasses of the plains just as the kwitu. They could not live confined in a wall garden of a city tower."

"But at the holdings they could? One could ride them where now only the sky ships pass overhead?"

Toph were certainly getting the point fast, perhaps almost too fast. But the off-worlder replied with the truth.

"That is so. A lord or the guardsman of a lord could ride across the country without slave bearers or a sky ship. My own world is plains and for hundreds of years have we so ridden—to war, to the hunt, to visit with kin, to see far places."

Toph looked down at the plate once again. "This is a new thing. The High One may be amused. I take." His thick fingers closed about the tri-dee with a grip of possession Kade did not try to dispute. The Terran had taken his first step in his plan, and by all signs Toph was snared. Surely the head animal keeper of the Pac would have some influence with the Lord of Cor, and the acquisitiveness of a zoo keeper faced with a new animal of promising prestige would be a lever in the Terran's favor.

When the Overman left without any further demands for information about the newly arrived bear, his hand still grasping the tri-dee, the Team Commander, who had taken no part in the exchange, smiled faintly.

"Why horses?" he asked.

"This is natural horse country. The plains will support them."

"You will have to have proof of that, an analytical report, before the Service will ship them."

Before he thought, Kade replied, "Steel had that made."

"Interesting," Abu commented. "You found that in his tape, of course. Horses—" he repeated thoughtfully. "They'd come high on import price."

"Too high?"

"For the High-Lord-Pac of a planet to indulge a whim? With all the resources of Klor to draw on? No, I think he can afford them if he wishes to. You might get a reprimand from the ecology boys however."

Kade had not forseen that angle. To introduce to any alien world a plant, animal, or bird without natural enemies and with a welcoming terrain was a risky thing at best. To Kade the plains of Klor seemed a natural setting for horse herds. They would share those vast expanses with the kwitu, with the deer species, and with the large flightless birds. Natural enemies—well, beside mankind, or Styor and Ikkinni, who should consider horses prized possessions and not prey, there were several carnivores. But none in quantity. Yet that was what he had hoped to see; a horse population exploding as it had on the plains of his own home, unleashing wealth and war mobility for the natives. However, if he had to untangle red tape within his own Service—

Kade was startled by a sound from his superior which was suspiciously like a chuckle.

"A little too soon, Whitehawk. Don't ride your rockets up full blast until you are sure of your orbit! Horses for the Styor. I wonder how the Ikkinni will welcome them. The currents of air keep their lords' ships out of the mountains. On horseback their slavers could range more widely. And I wonder about that, young man. You did not join this Team recommended as a Styor lover. Horses—" He studied Kade as a man might inspect an intricate piece of machinery which he did not understand, but must be able to set working with smooth ease.

"You said to tempt the High-Lord-Pac with something new," Kade said, on the defensive. He had been so full of his idea that he had underrated the Commander, a mistake he could see might be a disasterous error.

"So I did, so I did. And Steel, asking for an analysis, put all this into your mind?"

That was partly true and Kade was glad he could admit it. But he knew that Abu was not wholly satisfied. For the moment he was saved by the return of Toph with an order for them both to attend the High-Lord-Pac.

When they entered the antechamber of the garden where they had earlier deposited the bear, they found the ruler of Klor, his carrying-chair grounded, viewing the tri-dee which a guard held at eye level for his master's convenience.

"Tell of these." The order was passed to Kade.

Using the Trade tongue, the Terran enlarged upon equine virtues, giving what he hoped were vivid and entrancing descriptions of appearance, action, the advantages of horses to be bred and raised on Klor. There was no answering enthusiasm visible in the Styor, though it was plain the waiting Toph was already a convert.

"But in Cor they could not be?" The Styor interrupted.

"That is so. They must have open land."

"And the great ones of your world ride upon their backs with ease?"

"That is the truth." He launched into a description of saddles and riding gear, of the development of cavalry, both as fighting units and as striking and colorful guards for ceremonial occasions.

"These shall be bought," the Styor made his decision in his usual expressionless way. "Also there shall be sent to Cor reports concerning these creatures, other representations of them such as this, or larger." He gave the faintest inclination of head to the plate before him. "All this shall be done as speedily as possible."

Abu bowed. "The will of Pac is the law of the land and sky," he replied with the formal speech. "As the wish, so is the action. Have we now leave to depart from Cor, since we must carry out the will of Pac?"

"Depart and serve."

It was so quickly decided that Kade almost distrusted his success. On the way back to the Styor ship Abu asked some questions of his own.

"Where are you going to get horses in a hurry? When Pac says he wants a thing speedily, he means just that. Horses brought from Terra will be months on the way, and in quarantine and transhipment as well."

"There are horses, for generations toughened by space hopping, to be had on Qwang-Khan." Not his horses, the blooded breed of the Terran plains, but another stock, tough, wiry, inured to new worlds, developed from ponies which had once carried Tartar horsemen not only into battle, but on treks to challenge the rule of a quarter of the world.

"You've already done your research on the subject, I see." Abu again came uncomfortably close to the truth. But to Kade's relief, he pried no deeper.

CHAPTER 7

KADE AWOKE with that same feeling of present danger which had instantly aroused him into full awareness in the mountains. Yet behind him was the wall of his room at the post, beneath him the easi-foam of his bunk. He lay, schooling his breath to the even lightness of sleep, trying to catch sound or movement.

The window slit giving on the corridor was a lighter oblong against the dark wall. He heard the feather-light scuttle of a hunting "eight-legs" crossing the surface Then he caught a small sigh of breath released.

Another scurry from the "eight-legs", followed by the faintest of tiny squeaks as the Klorian creature captured one of the furry night moth-things. Then, from the courtyard, the sound of boots; sharp taps, rapping on the door of his senses.

A figure slid along the wall and the brush of passing was clearly audible. Whoever shared his room was almost within reach. He caught a trace of odor and knew that an Ikkinni crouched there, perhaps torn between the peril of the supposedly sleeping Terran by his side and the patroler in the courtyard.

Kade sighed as might a disturbed sleeper, rolled over so as to bring his forearms under him, ready to impell him off the bunk. Again he heard that catch of breath, felt rather than saw ruddy eyes fast on him. He had no idea of how keen Ikkinni night sight was, and he could take no chances. Though

67

the post natives were supposedly unarmed, there were objects within this very room which could be improvised into deadly weapons.

With one hand the Terran drew his stunner from the night pocket of the bunk and threw himself floorward, rolling over, to come up with his back against the opposite wall, the weapon ready. And he heard a flurry of movement from his invisible visitor, movement checked as the other laid hand on the door panel. For outside those parading boots still tapped a message of danger.

Then Kade had his answer to the amount of night sight possessed by an Ikkinni. Before he could move another body crashed against his and a hairy shoulder dug into his middle, driving the air from the Terran's lungs, smashing him back against the wall with a force which half dazed him so that he was helpless against a second attack. A blow on the side of the head crumpled him to the floor, barely conscious, and a second brought with it complete darkness.

"Whitehawk!"

Pain was a red band behind his blinking eyes, a light adding to it. His head rolled loosely as someone tried to pull him up, and he tasted the flat sweetness of blood. Then, somehow, fighting the swift stab of hurt in his head, he focussed his sight on Che'in. For once the other Trader was not smiling, in fact a very unusual grimness tightened the corners of his lips, brought into line the jaw structure which lay beneath the soft flesh of his round chin.

Kade's hand went uncertainly to his head and he winced when his fingers touched raw, scraped skin above a welt. They came away sticky red.

"What happened?" he asked huskily.

Che'in's arm slipped behind his shoulder, supported him so that he looked about a room which had been ripped apart. Every cupboard panel was open, forced where they had been thumb sealed. The foam of the bedding frothed through numerous rents in its outer skin, and a trail of record tapes crossed the top of the desk, ending in a confused pile on the floor. The evidence was that of a mad search, a search where the fury of the searcher had mounted with his inability to locate what he sought.

That could mean only one thing—or perhaps two!

Kade fought waves of dizziness as he tried to raise his head higher to survey more closely the debris on the floor about him. His boots were still standing at attention at the foot of the bunk. And noting they were undisturbed he knew that one secret had been safely kept.

"Stunner!" He cried. "Where is my stunner?"

If his assailant was Dokital and the native had his weapon—Why, an attack on Buk using the stunner might well mean death for half the Ikkinni slaves at the post. And whether that sacrifice was willing or not, Kade must prevent it by telling someone the full story.

Che'in pulled a familiar object from under Kade's leg. And the younger man snatched at it with a second wave of pure relief blanketing out the pounding in his skull for a welcome instant or two.

"I don't think your untidy friend will be back," Che'in remarked. "Have you any idea of what he was hunting for?"

To answer that meant danger of another kind. Again Kade stared at his boots. No one could possibly guess what had been cached in their concealed top pockets. And his head hurt so that his thinking was fuzzy.

"Wait!" Che'in edged Kade's head forward delicately, gently, making an examination, not of the welt left by the blow, but of the other's scalp lock. "So. When your visitor did not find what he wanted—" the Trader's breath came out as a hiss and again all lazy good humor was wiped from his features.

"What's the matter?" Kade put up his own hand, felt for the customary short braid. But his fingers discovered only a ragged tuft left. He had been hastily shorn by the thief. "Why?" Groggily he looked to Che'in for an answer.

Kade could understand the search for the remnants of the control which was still crumbling to smaller pieces in spite of his careful wrapping of the bits. And he could have understood the disappearance of the stunner. But why had the thief overlooked the weapon to take a few inches of human hair? The motive for that baffled him completely though he guessed it was clear to Che'in.

"The ordeal of the knots," the other spoke as if thinking aloud. "He did not find what he sought, so he would practice the ordeal of knots. But why? What did he seek here? This is important, Whitehawk. It may be deadly. Something Steel or you had?"

Kade took refuge in a collapse which was not more than a quarter acted, heard Che'in call out, and lying limp with closed eyes, heard the answering pound of feet. From his feigned faint he must have slipped into real sleep, for when he awoke again he was in the small post infirmary with the bright sheen of sunlight across the foot of his cot. They had probably drugged him for he discovered that thinking was a foggy process when he tried to put together into some sensible pattern the events he could remember.

What connection did those events have? He was almost certain Dokital had been his attacker. Since Kade's return from Cor he had seen almost nothing of the young Ikkinni, and a few offhand questions had told him that the native had been on a second hunting trip as Santoz's attendent. Kade's conscience had been none too easy. Out in the hills Dokital could put his dangerous knowledge to the rescue of another party of slaves. So the Terran had been relieved when the party had returned the day before, intact, and with an unusually good catch of musti in the bargain. If the Ikkinni had passed on his information, the natives had had no chance to steal a stunner and act upon it.

Unfortunately Kade was no nearer his own solution of how

to have the broken control box investigated. The technical knowledge such an examination would require was completely out of his field and he had no contact at the nearest Trade Base who could make such a study and subsequently keep his mouth shut. To approach the Commander here was simply asking for his own dismissal. And with his plan beginning to work Kade could and would not jeopardize his service on Klor. The order for horses had gone through to Qwang-Khan and been approved. Horses were on their way to Klor. And he had already made a start with his project of introducing the Ikkinni to what might be their future secret weapon of liberation.

On the very plausible argument that horses could not be transported to their final destination by Styor planetary freighters, but would have to be driven or ridden overland, Kade was conducting a lecture course for the post Ikkinni in the care, feeding and nature of the new arrivals-to-be. Tri-dees blown up to almost life size served to make familiar the general appearance of the off-world beasts. And, with the aid of an improvised structure of wood and tubing, Kade had demonstrated some of the points of riding, the nature of a saddle pad, and the use of reins in governing the mount. The imported mounts would naturally be already well trained and docile, at least considered so by their Terran breeders. But Kade still had no way of telling whether horse and Ikkinni could and would learn to live together.

To his disappointment so far he had awakened no visible reaction in the natives. Herded to the place of instruction by Buk, who watched and listened himself with close attention, none of the slave laborers appeared to consider lesson time more than an interlude of rest, enduring the Terran's efforts at teaching as the price which must be paid for such a breathing spell. With Buk there Kade had to keep closely to the text concerning the welfare of the off-world animals, imported directly for the pleasure and benefit of the Styor which the Ikkinni so hopelessly hated.

He had been pleased to see Dokital in his audience at the last class meeting. Somehow Kade had expected a more alert response from the native who had been attracted by the bear. But the young Ikkinni had proved as stolidly unresponsive as his fellows.

And now, with a faint ache still behind his eyeballs when he tried to focus upon the band of sunlight, Kade was discouraged enough to admit that Dokital wanted just one thing, release from bondage. Undoubtedly he believed the Terran had that in his power to grant but would not.

He had not found and plundered the hidden pockets in Kade's boots, nor taken the stunner. Why had he taken most of the off-worlders short braid? As far as Kade knew there was no Ikkinni custom demanding that to disgrace an enemy. And what possible use could Dokital find for about three inches of alien hair?

What had Che'in said? "Ordeal of the knots." Kade repeated that aloud now, but the words meant nothing.

"Yes."

Kade turned his head on the foam support. Che'in was well within the door, walking with a cat's silence in spite of his boots. There had been a subtle alteration in this Teammate, no direct change of feature, or real disappearance of the basic placidity Kade had always seen the other display. Only now the Terran knew that serene expanse as a mask, under which a new pattern was coming to life.

The other stood looking down at Kade thoughtfully.

"Why do they hate you, Whitehawk?" He might have been inquiring about the other's health, only he was not.

"Who?"

"The Ikkinni," Che'in paused, and then there was a slight difference in his tone. "So you *don't* really understand after all! But then what a disappointment, what a grievous disappointment." He shook his head slowly.

"For whom?" Kade bottled his irritation. Trying to get

any concrete information out of Che'in would seem to be a project in itself.

"The Ikkinni. And, of course, the Three Times Netter they employed to work on you. Or perhaps they have even hired a four knot man. From the disaster area they—or he—made of your quarters, I am inclined to believe your visitor was angry enough to go to a Four Netter—"

"Make sense," Kade's headache was returning. He was not amused by Che'in's riddle within riddle conversation.

"Magic," Che'in leaned back against the wall as if his usual indolence had caught up with him. "Take a tuft of an enemy's hair, knot it—with all the proper incantations and sacrifices—then each day draw those knots a little tighter—to be followed by subsequent bodily discomfort on the part of him whose personality is safely netted in your string of knots. If he agrees to your proposition, or you change your mind, certain of those knots can be untied again and his 'other self' released. If you get really thirsty for his blood, you tie your last knot firmly in a tangle and throw your net into a fire, or bury it in the earth, or dispose of it in some other final fashion which would provide a suitably unhappy end for your victim. Knotting is a local science of sorts I have been told."

Kade summoned up a grin. "And they expect this local magic to work on an off-worlder?"

Everyone knew that no one could be trapped by hallucination magic in which he was not conditioned from his birth. Yet the thought that somewhere a section of hairs, clipped in anger from his skull, was being skillfully and prayerfully knotted for the purpose of pain and revenge was not a pleasant one. Nor did it grow any less ominous the longer Kade considered it. Also there was always the chance that the hidden enemy, impatient at the ill success of his chosen scheme, might attack in a more forthright manner.

"If they discover their mistake," Che'in echoed Kade's last thought, "they may take more drastic, and quicker, steps.

73

Why *do* they hate you, Whitehawk? What really happened during that mountain trip of yours?"

Kade was being forced into the position where he had to take someone into his confidence. If he went to Abu he believed he would be summarily shipped off planet. The Team Commander could not possibly overlook his subordinate's flagrant violation of Service orders. But Che'in—could Kade trust him? They had nothing in common, save their employment at the same post, and the younger man knew very little of the other. In the end it was Che'in who made his decision for him.

"Lik was not killed by a kwitu."

Kade stubbornly held silent, setting his will against the silent and invisible pressure the other was somehow exerting.

"Lik came to a doubtlessly well-deserved end by violence, maybe a spear."

Kade was quiet as Che'in in his careless voice picked for the truth.

"Somehow, somebody discovered that a belt control is not entirely infallible."

Kade had schooled himself to meet such a guess. He was sure he made no move, not so much as a flicker of the eyelid, to reveal how close that hit. Yet Che'in was on it instantly. The difference which the younger Trader had noted in the other at his entrance was nakedly eager, breaking through the mask. Che'in looked alive as Kade had never seen him. The face was not that of a Trader, a man who lived by the Policy, but that of a warrior being offered a weapon which would make all the difference in some decisive meeting with an old enemy.

"That is the truth! Say it, Whitehawk! That is the truth!"

And Kade's will broke down under that flash of real emotion.

"Yes."

"No wonder they're after you!" Che'in's head was up, that avid eagerness still in his features. "If there is an answer to the collar control every Ikkinni on this planet will want it." He took a step forward, his hands closed firmly on the foot of the infirmary cot. "What sort of a game have you been playing, Whitehawk?"

"None." Kade hastened to deny what might be termed trickiness. "Everything was an accident. Lik was trampled, gored by that bull just as I said. What happened afterwards was pure accident." He retold the scene with the terseness of an official report.

"A stunner?" Che'in repeated wonderingly, drawing his own weapon from its holster. Then he added a sharp-toned demand. "What was your beam quota at the time?"

Kade searched memory. "Must have been on full. I hadn't thumbed down since I shot the kwitu."

"Full! And it blasted the control and scrapped the collars!"

"And killed two Ikkinni," Kade reminded him.

"Suppose the quota had been on lower voltage?"

"Well," Kade began and then stared warily at Che'in, suspicious of being led into some statement which would damn him irrevocably. "There is no way of experimenting on that score. The Styor certainly are not going to let off-worlders play about with a slave control box for the purpose of discovering how such can be made harmless."

"Correct." Che'in was masked again. He stood weighing his stunner in his hand as if he would like to try such an experiment. "However, there is this also, Whitehawk. That sonic was tampered with and you were meant to be the victim, just as Steel was written off the rolls earlier. It is good for us here at the post to know a few things, to prevent other bright ideas from overwhelming the ones who dreamed that one out of hyperspace—"

"Why do they—whoever they may be—want me—us—dead?"

Che'in smiled. "An excellent question and one to which there could be several answers. First, a great many of these petty lordlings dislike Terrans merely for being Terrans. We are the first threat to their status which has risen in the long, comfortable centuries during which they have had the large part of the habitable galaxy in their own tight pocket. Just to eliminate some Terrans under a safe and innocent cover would be sport enough to appeal to certain of our unfriendly acquaintances. Then there is the rivalry between the lords here on Klor. A few judicious 'accidents,' the cause of which might be attributable to the negligence of the slaves of one Styor by his jealous neighbor, would make a difference when the next season's hunting rights were allotted. A dangerous game, to be sure, but greed often spurs one into taking bigger risks than the prize warrants."

"But," Kade said slowly, "there could be a third possibility?"

"Politics," Che'in reholstered his stunner, leaned once more against the wall. "The game of Styor against Styor on Klor is also carried on at higher levels. It could be planet Viceroy against planet Viceroy, jockeying for power within their empire. This is an outpost and the officials here are in two catagories, the exiles with a black mark against them on the roles back home, and those who are ambitious but without power or backers. The first group want a coup to redeem their careers, the latter a chance to push their names. And use of carefully manufactured 'incidents' can help either."

"But too many Terran deaths—"

"Yes, if anyone is setting up that particular orbit he is locking his jets on danger, two strikes against his three-fin landing again. But some men are desperate enough for a tricky gamble. Someone, say, trying to unset the High-Lord-Pac."

"What are you going to do?" Kade came bluntly to the point.

"About this stunner business? Nothing just now. We need the raw material for an experiment. You still have the remains of the blasted control box?"

Kade nodded.

"That goes off the planet today, the supply ship is due in.

That fact, by the way, is what brought me here, Whitehawk. Someone has really humped himself passing papers hither and thither. Your precious oat-burners are on board."

Kade had swung his feet off the cot and was looking about for his clothing, the pain in his head forgotten. Che'in laughed and handed him his uniform tunic.

"They're not sitting on the landing apron yet. You have about four hours grace, since they are still in orbit. You needn't run *all* the way to the field—and don't forget that control box, friend."

Kade bent down, unseamed those lining pockets in his boot tops and brought out the four small packets into which he had divided the remains of both collar and control box, some of it now only metallic dust. If the experts could make anything out of these bits and pieces he would be not only gratified but amazed. And giving the responsibility of that task to Che'in left him freer in mind as he went to the field where he found most of the post personnel waiting. Some of his enthusiasm must have spread outwards to the others after all.

There were five mares and a stallion. Although not the proud, sleek creatures of Kade's dreams—for the imports from Qwang-Khan were smaller, shaggier in coat—all were dun with black manes and tails, their legs faintly marked with dark stripes, reverting to their far off Terran ancestors. But when the young Terran personally freed them from their shipping boxes, led them, still dazed from trip shots, out into the corral he had had built, Kade was pleased to find fortune with him. Against the general ocher-brown of the landscape they would be hardly visible from a distance. And these ponies used to the hardy life of one frontier planet would make an easier adjustment to another.

The Terran's only worry was the attitude of the Ikkinni. Since he had chosen to handle the animals himself upon their landing, Kade had not at first been aware of the fact that the natives did not approach the corral at all. Only later, when he wanted help in feeding and watering the new arrivals, he met Buk, and the latter had a sly half-grin.

"Does the starwalker want a labor gang?"

"The animals need water, food—" Kade stopped speaking as he saw Buk's fingers seek the control box, touch buttons which meant punishment for the slaves.

"Why?" Kade demanded, knowing that the Overman was enjoying this.

"These earth worms say those are devils starwalker brought to devour them. Unless they are driven they will not tend the horses."

"No!" If Buk drove the Ikkinni to handle horses under the lash of collar pain, Kade's plan would be defeated.

"I will lead the horses to the wide field," he said swiftly. "Let the Ikkinni then put the water and feed into the corral while it is empty."

Buk's grin faded. Kade allowed him no time for protest as he hurried to the corral gate. So far he had merely postponed trouble, but for how long? And was Buk telling the truth, or using his own power to make the natives hate and fear the horses?

CHAPTER 8

"That's it, not one of them will willingly go near the horses," Santoz sounded as if he were relishing Kade's discomfiture. "This situation could blow up into real trouble."

"If," Abu answered from the head of the council table, "we don't fulfill our contract with the Pac we'll also be in trouble."

"What I am asking," Che'in struck in mildly, "is how this 'devouring demon' rumor ever got started in the first place. We've imported other, and much more potentially dangerous

78

beasts in the past and never aroused more than some curiosity. Why this sudden antipathy for horses?"

Kade wanted an answer to that himself. It was almost as if someone—or something—had picked the *plan* out of his brain and set about an effective counterattack even before he had a chance to get started.

"Those other animals were smaller," Santoz pointed out with irritating reasonableness. "The only large animals native to Klor—the kwitu and the susti—are dangerous."

"So is the farg and that is just about the size of a half-grown bear. These Ikkinni were hunters before they were captured, we don't have any of the slaves from the breeding pens here. No, I would say that the rumor of demons did not spring full born from one of their crested skulls. I'd say it was planted."

"But why?" demanded Santoz.

Che'in smiled gently. "Oh, for any number of reasons, Manual. Say that such a story could be used to inflame the post laborers into a revolt—"

Santoz sneered. "Revolt! With Buk having their lives under his finger tips every second of the day and night? They're not fools?"

But, Kade's own thoughts raced, *a revolt with a method of handling Buk and his box, however risky, was possible. Was this the time to make a general confession?* His lips parted but Che'in was already speaking.

"I don't believe that any of us are experts in Ikkinni psychology. The Styor have not encouraged such research. Perhaps our best move—"

Abu cut in. "Our best move, since we can not lift a contracted order off-world again, is to get these animals into Styor hands as quickly as possible."

Che'in grinned. "Give the 'demons' into the keeping of those already granted such propensities by the Ikkinni. But, of course!"

That made good sense according to trade reasoning, yes. But Kade did not want a fast move in that direction.

"We'll have to take them overland," he pointed out. "And if the Ikkinni have to be forced to act as drivers—"

Abu frowned. "Yes, they might turn against the animals. Well, have you anything helpful to contribute?" His glance to Kade was direct, cold and demanding.

"Let me have one native to begin with, and no Buk. Two days of work about the corral may bring us a convert."

"I don't see how!" Santoz objected. "Any native would have to be collar-shocked to get him there and, without Buk, he could turn on *you*."

"You have someone in mind?" Abu asked.

"Well, there is Dokital. He asked questions about the bear. He might just be interested enough in horses to stay around until he saw that they weren't dangerous."

"Buk is interested in them," Santoz suggested.

Kade's hands tensed under the edge of the table. Santoz was right, the Overman had hung about the corral, asked a multitude of questions. But he was not going to take any cross-country ride with Buk as a partner.

"Not practical," Abu's retort had the snap of an order. "Unless we also choose to send along the labor force in its entirety. We can not use the Ikkinni here without Buk. The Lord Sabatha would withdraw all of them immediately. They're his possessions, ours only on lease. I don't know, Whitehawk, why you think you might have any luck with Dokital, but you can try for another day or so."

Only they were not to have another day. They were to have less than five hours.

Kade was in the field beyond the corral. He had a light riding pad on the stallion, another on the back of the lead mare. Equine nature had not changed across the star lanes, nor through the centuries. The herd was as it had always been; a wise mare to lead the bands into new pastures, the stallion ready to fight for his mares, bringing up the rear while in flight, nipping at those who fell behind.

By the gate of the corral stood a black figure, every line of his thin body suggesting, even from this distance, defiance he dared not translate into explosive action. Kade swung up easily on the stallion, booted the horse into a trot back towards the pole wall. And he did not miss Dokital's answering crab-wise movement which was halted only by the half-open gate. Now the Ikkinni stood penned as the horse and rider approached him, his hands opening and shutting as if searching the empty air before him for a weapon which did not materialize. The stallion stretched out his head, sniffed at the native, and blew gustily.

"The beast carries no spear against it," Kade said. "Across the star paths this beast serves warriors, wearing no collar but this," he lifted his hand, displaying the reins. "As the Kwitu, grass is for its eating, not the flesh of men."

The hostility he was certain he read in the native's eyes did not diminish. Kade knew, that with time pressing he must force matters. He whistled, the stallion nickered, and across the field the lead mare answered inquiringly. He had taken the precaution of looping her reins to the empty saddle pad, and now she came at a canter to join them, her sisters drifting after.

Buk was nowhere in sight, but Kade could not be sure that the Overman was not watching. Should the alien use the collar controls now— At least after his first attempt at escape Dokital had not moved, although Kade left a way open for him.

"Warriors ride," the Terran remarked. He put out his left hand and drew his fingers down the mare's soft nose.

"There is no warrior." For the first time the Ikkinni spoke. "It wears the collar." The heat of anger was searing, though the native did not even glance toward the stunner at Kade's belt.

"That is perhaps so," Kade agreed. "A warrior fights with a spear, a slave with magic knotted by night."

Dokital gave no answer to that charge. He stepped out of his corner refuge as if he were being pushed toward the horses and the rider by his desperate need to learn some truth. "The net holds it not?"

"The net is of Klor, how could it hold it which is not of Klor?"

Dokital blinked as he digested that bit of simple logic. But he had intelligence enough to not only accept Kade's answer but come back with a counter-argument to cross as a fencer's blade crosses his opponent's.

"The beast is not of Klor, how then can such be slave to those on Klor?"

"There is magic, and magic. Some kinds sweep from star to star, others bind the men of one world only. There is nothing to be learned without trial. The knots were netted for it, and that was a trial. Now let another trial be made."

For a moment, a very long moment, there was silence. Kade heard the ripple of breeze through the grass, the distant call of a sky high bird. He loosed the mare's reins, gathered them into his own hand.

Dokital moved, raising his palm up and out, taking one step and then another toward the mare. She turned her head, regarded the Ikkinni placidly. Then her nose came down to lip the native's fingers and Dokital stood valiantly, a tremor visible up his arm, yet he stood.

"Up!" Kade ordered, with a rasp which might have come from Buk's lips.

If Dokital had not appeared to absorb the information of the impromptu class in horsemanship it was surface indifference only. He mounted the mare clumsily. But he was safely on the riding pad when Kade walked the stallion out into the open land, leading the mare, the other horses trailing.

The walk became a cautious trot and the mare pushed a little ahead, until Ikkinni and Terran were riding almost thigh to thigh. Kade could read no expression on the native's face, but he was certain a measure of the other's rigid tenseness had vanished. And now Kade dared to increase the pace to a canter. They circled, were heading back toward the clustered buildings of the post, and Kade cut the speed back to a walk.

"A warrior rides," he said.

Dokital's hand went up to the collar he wore. "There is no warrior wearing this, starwalker," his head came around, his eyes were again red flames of eagerness. "Break these from us and you shall see warriors! But this must be soon."

A note in that alerted Kade. "Why?"

"The word has been passed. These are evil." Dokital combed his fingers in the mare's cropped mane. "There is said kill, kill!"

"Who kills? Those of the collars?"

"Those of the collars. With more from beyond." Dokital pointed with his chin toward the land which cupped the Terran post. There was the scarred landing apron, the winding river, the drifts of fast-growing grass broken by groves of trees, but it was a land at peace as far as Kade could see.

"From beyond?" he echoed.

Again, not lifting his hands from the mare's neck, Dokital gestured with his head toward the river.

"There are hunters out there. The Overmen bring them to a killing."

Kade reined in the stallion, leaned over as if to examine the rein lying along the horse's neck. But instead his eyes went on to the river bank. Not too close to the post one of the small bat-winged flying lizards zoomed to what must be the extent of its limited flight range. And it headed, not along the course of the waterway, but into the prairie. For the first time the Terran heard a sound near to a chuckle from the Ikkinni at his side.

"They walk there like the kwitu."

"Hunters?"

83

"That?" Dokital spat accurately over the mare's head, his opinion of such clumsiness in the stalk so made graphic. "No. One who drives."

"How many?"

"One who drives—six—eight—ten." The native recited the listing of belt controls indifferently. "Another who drives more, more." His crested head turned on his neck as he conveyed the idea that the post was now ringed by unseen enemy.

"But why?"

"Over many say starwalkers bring demons. It fears. Also Overmen drive."

And the Overmen could only be taking orders from the Styor! The stallion obeyed Kade's reining, the pressure of his knees. Out of the grass, between them and the walls of the post courtyard, arose a line of men. And from the post Kade heard a shout—perhaps of warning, perhaps of outrage and surprise. Small figures boiled out of hiding, ripped loose from the grove, erupted from the face of the prairie. There was no time to reach the control of the post's force field. Kade could hear a distant clamor which argued that a fight had already broken out inside.

He booted the stallion into a dead run, flattened himself as small as he could on the animal's back.

The war cries came from all directions and a spear, too hastily thrown, arched over the Terran's back.

"Slay. Slay the demons!"

This time the spear scored Kade's shoulder, ripping the stuff of his tunic, its passage marked by a smarting red line. But he had broken through the line of natives which came apart, curling away from his mounted charge. He was by the corral, almost into the courtyard.

A red Terran coat made a splotch of color by the drab wall of the com room. But the man who wore it was propped on his arms, coughing out his life, as a spear shaft danced between his shoulder blades. Kade drew his stunner, sent one Ikkinni crashing into the dying Terran.

Then, out of nowhere, a mesh wrapped about his head and shoulders, and he fought wildly against a net, trying to keep his seat on the saddle pad. The throttling cords gave a little as Kade jerked at them. Against him the mare crowded and a knee ground into his thigh as fingers caught at his wrist, forced the stunner out of his hold.

"Kill! Kill!"

Buk shouted the order from behind a barricade of bales. The Overman was sweating and there was an avid eagerness in his face. His fingers were on his control box, he must be driving his gang frenzied by those jolts of force. And a handful of the Ikkinni were battering at the door of the com room, using spear butts fruitlessly against a substance only a flamer could pierce.

The haired hand which had pried the stunner out of Kade's grip steadied, as the thumb clicked a new charge into place. Somewhere, somehow, the young Ikkinni had picked up the oldest rule of hand gun shooting; to aim it as one points a finger. And the finger now pointed to Buk's control.

Nothing outwardly marked the impact of that arrow of energy until Buk tottered against the bales, his mouth drawn into a square of pain, his hands pawing at the air, while the control box shattered in a bright burst of unleashed power.

But Buk was not finished. Perhaps mere blind fear and pain sent the Overman at Kade, the largest target in his vicinity. He threw his knife and the Terran, still half-pinioned by the net, had no defense. One of those same net ropes saved the off-worlder's life, deflecting that wicked point to score flesh but not wound deeply.

For the Terran the rest of the fight possessed a dream-like haze. Buk came on, wobbling uncertainly, his hands clutching air as if to tear at Kade. The Stallion backed, snorted, and ran. While Kade, one hand over the bleeding cut in his side, clung to the saddle pad with all his remaining strength. Nor was he aware that another rider followed, while the loose mares, scattered and running wild, eventually gathered to their leader to head for the hills where evening shadows were already standing long and dark.

Kade remembered only one other thing clearly. The scene came to him for the rest of his life as a small vivid picture.

The horses and their riders were already screened by rising river banks, but they followed the curve of the stream, so that Kade, as their gallop fell again to a trot, was able to witness the act of a Styor ship coming from the north. The flyer was not a freighter, but a needle-slim fighting ship, undoubtedly one of the Cor garrison.

It circled over the Terran post where the rising smoke told of continued destruction. Then, with an ominous deliberation the flyer mounted skyward vertically. The pilot's return to earth was slow, deadly, for he rode down his tail flames which crisped everything. Had any Terran survived the initial attack by the controlled natives, there was little or no hope for him now. Attackers and attacked alike had been burnt from the face of Klor. To Kade the callous efficiency of that counter-blast sealed the Styor guilt.

The Terran cried out, tried to turn the stallion back. But the reins were torn from his hold and, as a mist of pain and weakness closed in on him, Kade was dimly aware that they were headed on up the river into the mountains.

Arching sky over him was black, with the stars making frost sparkles across it, for the night was cold with the chill of early spring. Yet warmth and light were at his left, a warmth which was a cloak pulled over his half bared body. Kade dragged one hand across his left side, winced as its weight pressed a mass of pulpy stuff plastered on his wound.

He heard a low nicker, saw a horse's head, half visible in the limited light of the fire, toss with a flicker of forelock. And a figure came from the dark to loom over him. Dokital. Kade blinked, trying to see what was strange about the Ikkinni. A long moment later his dulled wits knew. The native's throat was bare, his slave collar was gone. As the other folded up his long legs to hunker down beside the Terran, Kade raised his hand.

"It is free."

White teeth flashed between dark lips. "It is free."

Those long-fingered hands went to work on Kade so he speedily forgot everything but the painful reaction of his body. The crushed mess was scraped from tender skin and a second poultice applied, patted into place with what seemed to Kade to be unnatural firmness. Unclenching his teeth he asked a question.

"We are in the hills?"

"The higher places," Dokital assented. "The collar masters can not come here. The Spearman brings down their fly-boats."

"And the post?" But Kade's memory already supplied the answer to that.

"There is no place. Those have left it only stinking earth."

Kade digested that. There was a chance, a very slim one, that perhaps Abu or Che'in, or both, *had* survived. He was sure that Santoz was the man he had seen die on the spear. Every Trade post was equipped with an underground emergency com. If the other two had managed to reach that in safety before the burn-off, there was a good chance they could hold out there until the help summoned by their SOS came. But the chance of such survival was indeed thin. Had they been above ground, still exchanging fire with the attackers when the Styor ship struck, then, he was the last Terran left on Klor.

Meanwhile, for him, the mountains where the Styor ships could not patrol were the safest hideout.

"The horses?"

"One died from a spear," Dokital reported. "But the rest ran—faster than the kwitu, than the slog, faster than any

Ikkinni, or any spear from an Ikkinni hand. Truly they are windswift ones!"

"Where do we go?"

Dokital fed a piece of rust-colored wood to the fire. "It is free. In the upper places there are many free warriors. It will be found."

"Iskug?"

"Iskug or others." He added a second piece of wood and the flames shot higher. Kade pulled himself up on one elbow, saw the horses stand, their heads pointing to the light, as if they, too, sought the promise of security, if not the warmth, of the fire.

But if Dokital meant that splotch of yellow-red in the night as a signal, there came no immediate answer. And at last the flames died, unfed, while Kade slept uneasily, but unstirring.

He awoke again cold, cramped, a chill slick of dew beading his good shoulder where he had pushed aside a light covering of twigs and lengths of dried grass. The throbbing in his side was only a faint memory, to be recalled when he moved stiffly to sit up. Last night's fire was burnt away to a handful of charred wood ends and a smear of ash. Seeing that, he looked around quickly, plagued with the thought he had been left in a deserted camp.

A sharp jerk jarred his wound into painful life again as he discovered that his feet were anchored, lashed together at his ankles, the ends of those bonds fastened out of sight and reach. The slab of vegetable plaster on his side flaked away as he leaned forward to pull at the cords. Certainly Dokital the night before had shown no signs of hostility. Why had he bound the Terran while he slept?

With a catch of breath at the hurt it cost him, Kade managed to finger the cords about his ankles. They were twisted lines such as were used to weave hunters' nets and he could feel no knots. The ends of the lines vanished between large boulders on either side, holding him firmly trapped. He remembered Che'in's talk of four fold knots to hold an enemy. But that had been a part of native magic. What he felt and saw here had very concrete reality.

CHAPTER 9

ABOUT HIS BOOTS the loops were tight and smooth almost as if they had been welded on. And their substance was not that of ordinary rope, for his fingers slid greasily around without contacting any roughness of braided surface. Kade raised his head, tried to gauge by the amount of light now gilding the peaks how far the morning had advanced. The hour was well past dawn, for sun touched the upper reaches.

Standing strongly against the sky were those three impressive peaks, the Planner, the Netter, the Spearman, which told him that their flight the day before had brought them in the same general direction as the hunt had taken weeks earlier.

Last night's camp had been made against the flank of a rise where the debris of an old landslip had set up a backwall of boulders. Kade caught the faint gurgle of water flowing swiftly, so a mountain stream could not be too far away. And that sound triggered his thirst. Suddenly he wanted nothing so much as to bury his face in that liquid, drink his fill without stint.

Kade could see the space where the horses had stood in the dark, watching the fire. But there was no sign of those animals now, just as Dokital had vanished. Had the Ikkinni taken them and gone for good?

The Terran writhed, and in spite of the pain which clawed at his side, drew his feet as far toward his middle as he could before kicking vigorously. The bonds gave a matter of inches and that was all. With his hands he dug in the loose soil and gravel beside and under him, discarding a length of charred branch, hunting a stone with which he could saw at those stubborn loops. If necessary he would try abrading them with handfuls of the gravel.

A first pebble was too smooth. Then he chanced on a more promising piece of rock, having a blunted point at one end. Pulling forward, his left arm protectingly across his wound, Kade worried at the cords. And rubberwise, those bonds resisted his determined assault.

Dripping with sweat, weak with effort and pain, Kade sat, shoulders hunched, the stone clasped in his hand. He was sure that an hour or more had passed since he had awakened, the sun was farther down the sundial of the mountain. And he was equally sure with the passing of time that he had been abandoned by Dokital, though why the native had taken the trouble of tending the Terran's wound before deserting him Kade could not understand. Unless the Ikkinni had left him staked either as an offering to the three stark mountain gods, or to be found by the pursuing Styor.

And the latter supposition sent Kade to a second attack on the ankle ropes.

The odor of the dried poultice, of his own sweat, was strong in his nostrils, but not strong enough to cover another scent. He became aware of that slowly, so intent was he on his own fight. The new stench was rank, so rank that he could no longer ignore nor mistake it. Kade stiffened, head up, nostrils wide.

Once that noisome odor had been sniffed, a man never forgot it. And the whiff he had had to plant its identity in his memory had come from a cured, or partially cured, hide back at the post. This was so ripely offensive it could only emanate from a living animal. Animal? Better living devil!

The musti of the caves were dangerous enough, they had claws to rend, fangs to threaten. But they had a cousin which was far more of a living peril, a thing which hunted by solitary tracking, which could spread wing or creep on all fours at will, with a man-sized body, a voracious hunger, an always unsatisfied belly. And because it feasted on carrion as well as live prey it aroused revulsion instantly. Kade cringed as he began to guess why he had been tethered here, though the reason behind that action still eluded him. It would have been far safer for Dokital to have used a spear and finished him off neatly and quickly.

That stench was now almost a visible cloud of corruption. But, though the Terran strained his ears for the faintest sound which might hint at the direction from which sudden death would come, he heard nothing save the sigh of wind through branches, the continuing murmur of that tantalizing stream. Only his nose told him that the susti must be very close to hand.

He squirmed around, jerking desperately at his bonds, managing to fight enough play into those ties so that he could pull himself up, put his back to a boulder. Half naked, with nothing but the stone in his hand, Kade looked around for another possible weapon. To his mind the outcome of the fight before him was already settled, and not in his favor.

His stunner was long gone, but he still wore the belt with its empty holster. Now Kade tore feverishly at the buckle, pulled the strap from around him. He held a belt of supple yoris hide, a buckle and the holster weighing down one end. And he twitched it in test, seeing that he could make it a clumsy lash of sorts. With that in his right hand and his stone in the left, the Terran pushed tight against the rock to wait for the lunge he was sure would be launched at him from one of three directions.

Straight across the ashes of the fire was an open space, the last path the susti would choose. The creature was reputed to be a wily hunter, and its species had been ruthlessly hunted by Ikkinni and Styor alike for generations. Stealth must have been bred into its kind by now.

To Kade's left the trail of debris made by an old slide made a gradually diminishing wall, a dyke of large and small boulders, rough, climbable, but not a territory to welcome a rushing charge. And anything crossing it would be plainly in view for several helpful moments before reaching him. The Terran hoped that would be the path. He held his head high, trying to test the odor for a possible direction of source.

His right offered the greatest danger. There was a curtain of brush some five feet away. He could see broken branches where Dokital must have raided for wood and for the covering he had heaped over Kade before leaving. But the vegetation was still thick enough to conceal a full squad of Ikkinni had the natives chosed to maneuver within its cover. Was it too thick to allow the winged susti passage?

Kade swung the belt back and forth, trying to get the feel of that unlikely weapon. He could use the strap as a flail, with the faint hope that the holster might thud home in some sensitive spot, say an eye. But that hope was so faint as to be almost nonexistent. And his head turned slowly from boulder wall to brush, striving to catch some betraying movement from the thing which must be waiting not too far away.

Such waiting gnawed at the nerves. The belt ends slapped against the Terran's breeches. Kade braced himself against the stone, struggled again to loosen the cording at his ankles. Free he might have a chance, a minute one, but still a chance. Then his heart thumped as one of the two anchoring lines gave so suddenly he was almost thrown. The cord rippled toward him from between two rocks. That side was free!

But he was to be given no more time. The susti had assured itself that this was not a baited trap. With a blast of roar, partly issuing from a crocodile's snout—if the crocodile had worn fur and possessed tall standing ears—and partly from the ear-storming claps of leather wings, the nightmare which haunted Klorian wilds burst through the brush and came towards Kade in a scuttling rush.

The Terran hurled his stone as a futile first line of defense, before swinging with the belt, cracking against the snout in a vicious clip. The talons, set on the upper points of the wing shrouded forelimbs, cut down. Somehow Kade ducked that first blow, heard the claws tear across the rock against which he had taken his stand. There was only the chance for one more blow with the belt. Again he felt and saw the improvised lash crack against the creature's snout. Then one of those wings beat out and Kade was pinned helplessly to the stone, his face buried in the noisome, vermin-ridden fur. One of the powerful back legs would rise, a single rake would disembowel him.

There was a squeal which was not part of the susti vocal range. Kade, his head still crushed by the wing, felt the creature's body pressed tighter against his as if impelled by some blow from behind. Then he was gasping fresh air, his hands rubbing his eyes, the susti's weight no longer crushing him.

With a speed he would not have believed possible to a creature so awkward on the ground, the Klorian terror had moved to face a new antagonist. Kade saw hooves flash skyward, come down in the cutting blows of axe-fatality. One such landed full on a wing, flattening the susti from a crouch to the sand. Before the creature could struggle up, the Terran stallion, squealing with red rage, brought punishing teeth to snap trap-tight on the nape of the susti's neck, tearing free only with a mouthful of flesh.

Kade had heard of the desperate ferocity of stallion fighting stallion for the kingship of a herd. Once he had seen such a duel to the death. And here was the same incarnate rage, the same deadly determination to win, turned not against a fellow horse, but against the alien creature.

The susti had been unprepared for that meeting, and it never recovered the advantage lost at the first blow. Since the stallion was able to rear above his enemy, using sharply shod front hooves as a boxer uses his hands, he repeatedly flattened the bat-thing, each fall of those weapons breaking bones, each rake of teeth ripping strips of flesh. Kade had never witnessed such raw and bloody work and he could hardly believe that the animal that had moved quietly under his orders could have changed in a matter of seconds into this wild fury.

Long after the susti must have been dead the horse continued to trample the body. Then all four feet were on the ground, the dun neck stretched so that distended nostrils could sniff at the welter of splintered bone, blood-matted fur. There was a snort of disgust from the stallion. He threw up his head, his black forelock tossing high, to scream the challenge of his kind triumphantly.

Kade tore at the last of the cords which held him, putting all his strength into that pull. The bonds yielded reluctantly but he was able to twist and turn the loops until he kicked free. The stallion was trotting away between brush wall and boulder and the man ran after him.

He found the horse, coat splotched with foam, a line of sticky red down one shoulder proving that the stallion had not come altogether unmarked out of that battle, with front feet hock-deep in the stream, drinking from the top curls of topaz water. There was a spread of meadowland, pocket-sized but rich in grass, on the other side of the water. But, contrary to Kade's expectations, it did not hold the mares.

The Terran moved up beside the horse. Again that head tossed, flicking droplets of water on Kade's arm and reaching hand, evading the man's touch. The horse still wore riding pad and the reins trailed loosely from the hackamore.

Kade hissed soothingly but the horse snorted, jerked away from the man's hand. It was then Kade realized he must still reek of the susti. Kneeling beside the streamside, well away from the horse, he pored cold water over head, shoulders, chest where that rank fur had smeared against his flesh. He felt the sting in his wound. Gritting sand rubbed away the last foul reminder of that contact. And now the horse allowed him close, to dab at that shoulder scratch with a soaked wad of grass. The furrow was not deep, Kade noted with relief. But the arrival of the stallion without the mares, with no sign of Dokital, continued to puzzle the man. And what had so aroused the horse to that attack against a beast which had not threatened him?

Kade had heard tales of horses and mules on his planet battling mountain lions, thereafter developing such an animosity against the big cats that they deliberately sought the felines out with a singleness of purpose and desire for vengeance against that archenemy of their kind. That was close to the reaction of a human under similar circumstances. Yet the stallion could not have met a susti before and Kade had not attempted to condition the animals since their arrival on Klor. Either unusually thorough precautions and preparations had been made off-world to acclimate the newcomers to all possible Klorian dangers, or the susti by its vile stench and very appearance had aroused hatred in the new immigrant. At any rate, Kade's life had been bought in that encounter and he was duly grateful.

The problem of what to do now remained. Where would they go? Leading the stallion, the man splashed across the stream and found what he had hoped to see; hoof prints cut in the soft clay of a sloping bank. If the traces continued as clear as this he would have no difficulty in back-trailing the horse and perhaps so discovering where Dokital and the mares had vanished.

Mounting, Kade headed the horse across the valley, pausing to study the trail now and then, each time seeing traces. Either the horses had left those while running free, or the Ikkinni had not taken the trouble to conceal the evidence of their passing.

The strip of meadowland narrowed, overshadowed by rising mountain walls, and the ground began to slope upward, gradually at first and then at a more acute angle. Kade revised his guess that the animals had taken that path of their own choosing. With water and good grazing in the valley, they would not voluntarily have picked such a way into the heights. Yet here and there a deep hoofprint marked either the exit of the small herd, or the return of the stallion.

Kade halted at the top of the rise to rest his mount and, with the age-old training of his kind, slipped from the pad, loosening the cinch to allow air to circulate under the simple saddle, before he crept to the edge of the downslope ahead, taking advantage of all offered cover.

The downslope was wooded, masked with a bristly cover of the twisted dwarflike trees found in the heights. Wind stirred through them, roughed Kade's flesh with its bitter bite. But more than wind moved on that curve of hillside. There was no mistaking the nature of those moving dots coming up with the dogged persistence of animals driven by a homing instinct. The mares! And none bore a rider.

Daringly Kade whistled and some trick of air current carried that summons to the sensitive ears below. The lead mare nickered and quickened pace, her sisters falling in behind her. Rocks rolled and behind Kade the stallion sounded his own call.

When the mares reached the ridge they were sweating, their eyes strained, showing white rims, their coats rough with dried foam and sweat, bits of twig and bark caught in the rippling length of their tails. By all the signs they had traveled far and fast.

The lead mare still wore the riding pad and her rein was caught to it on one side, dangling loose on the other. Also the pad was twisted and across its edge—

Kade put out a finger. That smear of blood, differing in shade from his own, was already partly congealed. The drop must have been exposed to the air for some time. But its presence there argued that there was a more sinister reason for Dokital's absence. Had the native been killed? But where? And why had he ridden the mare, driven the horses away, leaving Kade helpless in the deserted camp? Every time the Terran tried to make a pattern out of the bits and pieces he knew or suspected, they did not fit.

In the end he led the horses back to the valley of the camp, sure that they would be content there. The stream supplied him with the first food he had had that day; a fish, flat, elongated, almost unpleasantly snakelike, but one he knew was edible even raw, and he finished it off with the dogged determination to consume food as fuel for his demanding body.

The fish also supplied him with what he wanted almost as much as food; a weapon, or at least the beginnings of a weapon which, with some careful labor, would serve. The tough spinal bone, shorn of its fringe of small projections and sharpened, made a poniard, needle-slim and nearly as deadly as dura-steel.

How much that would serve him against a Styor blaster, or an Ikkinni spear, he questioned. But with it in his hand Kade felt less naked. And he worked at its perfection all that long afternoon as he made some plans of the future.

The Styor, after their ruthless attack on the Trade post, would hunt down any remaining off-world witness with speed and dispatch. Let his survival be suspected and they would have hunting teams into these breaks to comb him out, station squads all along the trails leading back to the post to pick him up. The logical move would be for him to contact the free Ikkinni, Iskug's band of escapees. That would have been his first endeavor yesterday, before he awoke bound and easy meat for a susti. Now he might have to fear the natives as much as he did their oppressors.

Yet a third possibility was so dangerous, that to try such action meant very careful planning, a period of scouting and lurking, of learning the countryside. To reach the destroyed post Kade would have to evade Styor patrols and natives alike. And even when he reached that site he might not be able to find the concealed com, or to summon the Service ship in time to save himself. But he could get out a warning of what had happened on Klor.

Kade ground with small, delicate touches at the point of his bone dagger. To scout the territory would commit him to no move and he should so be able to gauge the Styor positions. That much he would try tomorrow. He was fairly certain at the way west from here and he should be able to reach some upper vantage point in the hills from which to view the post by midday.

The Terran followed Dokital's example of the night before, heaping a loose pile of grass into which he crawled, listening to the movements of the horses until he fell asleep, knowing that they would give the alarm against alien intruders.

Kade awoke soon after dawn to hear the low whinny of the lead mare as she went down to the stream. He pulled free of his nest, went to the water also. Following the immemorial custom of hunt and war trail Kade drank only a small amount of water, pulling tighter the belt about his middle. As he swung past the boulder wall of Dokital's camp a gorged winged thing shuffled along the cleaned skeleton of the susti, and two smaller shapes turned angry red eyes on him before they scuttled away into hiding.

Taking his bearings from the three peaks, the Terran headed westward. He had to make detours around two unclimbable cliffs and paused now and again to erase the marks of his own passing. Slightly before midday he did reach his goal. As he crept along a ledge the sun was pleasingly warm on his shoulders and he did not regret the loss of his tunic. For against the hue of sand and earth here his own bronze skin and the drab shade of his breeches should be undistinguishable.

Although miles separated him from the post, there was no mistaking the scar which the Styor burn-off had left to mark the site. Not one of the walls still stood, only a round splotch of blackened earth gleamed under the sun, the terrible heat of the ship's flaming tail had cooked earth and sand into slag.

He could have hoped for nothing else. Had there been survivors, they must be sealed underground, their only hope of rescue to come from off-planet. Kade looked from that scar to more immediate landscapes. He had one small point in his favor, the Styor would expect a Terran to be completely bewildered if thrown on his own in the Klorian wilderness, and the Overmen of teams sent out to track any possible survivor would be overconfident.

That estimation of the enemy was borne out when Kade surveyed the foothills below his present perch. There were trackers out, right enough. He could sight two separate teams heading eastward, and they moved openly, strung out as might beaters sent to scare up game. There was no doubt that sooner or later someone down there would stumble on the trail left by the horses day before yesterday and follow it to the valley of the susti. Which meant he must move and find a better hideout.

But even as Kade started to crawl from his ledge, he stiffened, hearing that familiar clap of sound, the roar of a spaceship homing on a post land area. And, in the sunlight, the silver body of a descending Trade scout was a streak as vivid and elemental as an avenging bolt of lightning.

CHAPTER 10

IF KADE HAD BEEN startled by the sudden arrival of the Terran ship in Klorian skies, the search parties below betrayed their agitation by the speed with which they took to cover. Although he could no longer sight them, the off-worlder knew they still existed, a barrier between him and that ship now making a perfect three-fin landing on the apron of the vanished post. He had not the slightest chance of reaching the rescue party.

But he continued to watch their activities with strained eagerness. Would the Styor attempt to attack the party from the ship? Or would the aliens bring up one of their fast inter-atmosphere cruisers from Cor and begin a running fight when the Terran scout took off again? Kade did not see how they would dare to let the ruined post tell its story to Trade. Had the Styor not blasted, but allowed the evidences of a native attack to stand, they might have successfully blamed it on rebellious Ikkinni, indirectly on the Terrans themselves because of the importation of horses. As he lay there on the ledge, his head supported on his forearm, Kade thought that made good logic.

But why had they spoiled such a plan with the burn-off? What had gone wrong? Unless—unless they had learned of the blasting of Buk's control! Had the Styor lords, safely in the background of that assault, been able to monitor events from a distance and observed that the Ikkinni had a weapon of deliverance at last? Had they ordered the burn-off to catch their own dupes as well as the Terrans for no other reason than to make sure that no more stunners would fall into Ikkinni hands, than if they moved fast and were lucky, no rumor of the weapon's use could reach the rest of their slave gangs? It could be an answer, if a drastic one—risking a blockade from Trade in order to keep their slaves. But how could he judge the thinking patterns of a Styor by his own processes? The risk to them might have appeared heavier on the other side of the scales.

At any rate someone had been frightened enough, or angry enough to order that burn-off. Would the next attack come against the newly landed ship?

Minutes passed and no Styor flyer arose above the horizon. There was no sign of life from the breaks below where those hunting parties had gone to earth. Kade could make out, despite the distance, figures emerging on the ship's ramp, descending to the congealed scar of the post. And he speculated again as to whether Abu or Che'in was sealed, still alive, below the glassy surface of that burn.

Renewed activity below his perch drew Kade's attention away from the splotch on the prairie. There was a new advance, not back toward the plains, but up slope, heading towards him. And for a moment or two he wondered if he had been sighted and Ikkinni slaves dispatched to pick him up.

If the newcomers knew the terrain well they could take a

path around the spur on which he crouched, cutting him off. And Kade dared not chance that they were ignorant of that, too many labor gangs had been hired out for hunting in these hills. He had to leave at once.

The Terran gave a last long look at the scene about the ship. Those small stick things which represented his own kind had gathered in one spot on the scar. His guess that at least one of the Team was in a hidden underground com chamber must be right and they were preparing to break the prisoner out. Kade eyed the section of broken, wooded land below him, the long curve of open prairie. To try to cross those miles was simply asking to be speared—or blasted if the Styor had issued more potent arms to their Overmen. He had not the slightest chance of reaching the safety of the ship and that was a bitter truth to digest.

But suppose the scout took off successfully with the man or men who had been rescued? There would remain that now open com chamber and the possibility he could try for it later, send in his own call. That was the hope he must hold to as he retreated now.

Kade crept from his ledge, started downward with the ridge rising as a wall between him and the only aid he could count on, using every tactic known to a hunter—and the hunted—to cover his trail.

Once he wriggled under a fallen tree, lay still, fighting the rapid pump of his own heart, the rasp of his breathing, while an Ikkinni paused within arm's-length, head up, nostrils distended, as if he could pick out of the light breeze which was ruffling his cockscomb of hair the scent of the off-worlder.

Kade blinked when he saw that that particular tracker wore no collar. If the slave Ikkinni had been loosed in the hills, their free brethern were also on the move with a purpose which drove them into dangerous proximity to the Overmen and their governed squads.

The Terran watched the native fade into the brush, and lay long moments in hiding, until he was sure of a detour which would not bring him treading on the other's heels. So tangled a path did Kade follow that he was honestly surprised when he came again into the meadow where the horses grazed. And the hour was close to sunset as he stayed under cover watching the animals.

But the peace of the scene was reassuring, especially when the stallion betrayed quick vigilance with his own examination and then welcome for Kade. Had the Terran been Ikkinni or Styor he was certain the herd would have been in flight before the invaders could get within blaster range of the animals.

However, with hunters boring into the mountain valleys, man and mounts dared not remain there in spite of the coming night. Kade mounted the lead mare, headed her back along the trail he had explored the day before, and was glad that the others came behind willingly, the stallion playing rear guard.

The Terran pressed the pace, wanting to be over the rougher stretches of trail while the daylight lasted. But he paused every time they were forced out of cover to look behind. And he regretted he had no chance to erase their tracks.

They came back, in the gray of the twilight, to the wooded slope where earlier he had met the mares. And now the leader he rode whinnied nervously, had to be urged on. Yet Kade could see nothing but empty country below, and he was sure they had outdistanced the hunting parties. There remained the free Ikkinni, nor did he forget that blood which made an ugly blotch on the saddle pad not far from his knee.

He let the mare pick her own choice of ways as long as she obeyed his selection of direction. And she went cautiously, pausing to sniff the air, survey the unending ocher vegetation ahead. Once or twice the stallion snorted, as if growing impatient at that slow advance, but he did not press ahead.

Kade was hungry, as he could never remember having been since the ceremonial fasting of his adolescence, and here in the shadow of the trees he was cold as well. Sooner or later he would have to choose a camp site.

The mare stopped short, her ears pointed forward, and now the stallion joined her, his whole stance expressing interest in something hidden from Kade's less acute sense. There was nothing to be seen save the trees, the sparsely growing underbrush, and countryside being blotted out by dusk.

Then the breeze, which awakened a murmur of sound, failed and Kade caught a quiver in the air—it was hardly more than that. Only the rhythm of that faint beat was manmade, he became convinced of that the longer he listened. And surely the Styor hunting parties would not advertise their presence by such means.

A village or gathering of cliff Ikkinni? Some ceremonial in progress? Or— His imagination supplied other explanations. He pressed his heel against the mare's round side, urging her on. And, as she obeyed, that faint pulsation grew louder. Then some trick of shifting wind brought it to him as a regular up-down ladder of sound. And his blood answered that alien cadence with a faster coursing, his heart accelerated to keep time to that drumming.

Horses and man came out of the trees into a glade, and here the drum was a hollow core of vibration which pulled, not only at the eardrums, but at the nerves of the listener. The horses were uneasy, nickering. Finally the stallion reared, gave his ringing challenge as his front hooves beat into the sky. Kade caught for dangling reins too late, aware that that fighter's scream of defiance could carry, echoed as it was by the rises about them.

Yet there was no pause in the boom of drum or drums, no answering move in the shadows to indicate that the drummer was aware of strangers. And Kade knew that he must investigate the source from which that beat came.

He dismounted from the mare, tethered her by her reins, sure her sisters would not drift too far away. Then, trusting in the fighting powers of the stallion, Kade chose to ride the stud on, drawn by that rolling sound.

Luckily a measure of light still held. The horse struck into an easy canter which took them out over a stretch of bare earth pocked with scrubby plants, an abrupt contrast to the more luxuriant foliage of the upper slope. They came into a draw gouged out by some seasonal water gush but now dry, firm and smooth enough to ape a leveled road. The stallion's canter lengthened into a gallop. The horse shied as one of the long-legged wingless birds erupted from the right. But when the Klorian creature ran on straight ahead, Kade's mount appeared to accept that burst of speed from its strange racing companion as a goad and the stride of those powerful legs lengthened once again.

The drums were loud now, a continuous, thunderous roll. And perhaps they acted upon the horse with some of the same impact of which Kade was himself aware. But the man kept his head and tried to control his mount as a glow ahead told him he must be approaching the site of activity.

Running yards ahead of the stallion the bird uttered a mewling cry, gave a contorted sidewise leap which warned Kade. He loosened rein again, kicked the stallion into a bound, flattened himself as close as he could to the horse's back. There had been a shadow crouched in the dry water course, a figure which arose in a spring. The horse leaped and that shadow fell away with a cry of terror.

Now when Kade pulled at the reins he found that the horse was past obedience. Given time he might bring the stallion back under control, but for a time the Terran could only keep his seat and wait for this fury to run itself out.

Kade thrust his knees under the loose foreband of the pad, riding as had his ancestors during the excitement of a buffalo hunt on a world half the galaxy away, reasonably sure he would not lose his seat. As horse and rider rounded a curve in the stream bed, the glow brightened, shooting heavenward in two pillars of light.

Without his rider's urging, the stallion began now to curb his headlong rush as he drew closer to the fires, coming at last to an abrupt halt. As the horse reared, voicing a tearing scream, Kade knew his precautions against being thrown had been well taken.

And he guessed in part what might lie ahead for he would never forget that stench, a whiff of which came nauseous and pungent through the softer odor of smoke and burning wood. Somewhere behind the hazy gleam of those twin fires was a susti, either alive, or very recently dead.

At first those fires dazzled his eyes. Then, as the stallion advanced in an odd, sidling way, with suspicion and wariness in every move, the Terran caught the weird scene in its entirety.

Here some freak of nature had hollowed an almost perfect horseshoe-shaped amphitheater, three slopes rising from a bare floor of sand, the fourth open to the gorge down which Kade had come.

An audience filled those slopes, movement pulsated around the bend of the horseshoep with here and there a down-covered Ikkinni face brought into momentary sharpness as the flame pillars wavered. Yes, there was an audience; more natives than Kade had ever seen gathered in one place before. He pulled at the reins, to discover that the stallion would still not obey. Unless he dismounted he was going to be carried on into the channel of light between the fires.

Kade drew the bone knife, knowing the uselessness of that weapon against the spears which would meet him now.

With rein and voice he appealed to the stallion, hopelessly. For the horse was still sideling ahead, hooves moving in a dance of small advances, smaller retreats. Then the arched neck went down and a front hoof tore up a fountain of gravelly sand.

A figure moved at a point midway between the fires but still yards away from the two in the gorge. And Kade saw the focus of this entire assemblage.

An Ikkinni stood there, equipped with net and spear, though he held the net in his hands and the spear lay on the earth with one of his feet set upon its shaft. Kade's attention, caught by the wink of fire on that weapon's point, located a round ring of cord about the ankle of the waiting native; something he remembered well. This was a prisoner, his feet bound even as Kade's had been in the deserted camp. A captive and yet armed with the weapons of his people, tethered by his feet—

And the smell of susti!

The stallion advanced, his head still held at an awkwardly low angle, as if he were nosing out a trail which existed a foot or so above ground level. The steps the horse took were small, mincing, and Kade felt the roll of muscle between his own knees, sensed the power for attack building up there.

It was then that horse and rider must have been sighted for the first time. A cry, eerie, piercing, sounded from some point high up on the slope to Kade's left. He heard a chorus of answering hoots from the other half-seen sections of the amphitheater. The Ikkinni prisoner turned, crouching, and Kade saw him full face. Nor was he in the least surprised to see that the captive was Dokital.

How the former post slave had come here Kade did not know, but that he had been set in his present position for the amusement or edification of enemies of his own species was apparent. And the nature of the peril to be faced was more evident with every breath of tainted air which Kade drew.

Nor did the Terran doubt that the animal he bestrode had indeed been conditioned, either by nature or by off-world techniques, to seek out and attack the source of such a stench, a living susti.

The stallion continued his seemingly awkward advance toward Dokital. And the cries which had heralded the appearance of horse and rider abruptly died away. Nor did any spectator move to interfere with either Kade or his mount. Perhaps, thought the Terran savagely, taking fresh grip on his wholly inadequate bone knife with fingers which were sweat-sticky, they had settled to watch their entertainment increased threefold.

Dokital, after his first startled glance at the newcomers, half-turned from them again, his whole stance betraying preparation for action as he stared beyond the fires to the rounded curve of the horseshoe, plainly expecting danger from that direction.

The stallion was well into the firelight and Kade debated as to the wisdom of dismounting. He had seen the animal in successful action against one of the weird bat-things, and the weight of a rider might handicap the four-legged fighter. Loosening his knees from the pad, he leaned forward and stripped hackamore and reins from the horse's head. The head was up now, nostrils distended, small flecks of foam showing in frothy patches about the angle of the half open jaw.

Kade leaped down, landing a stride's distance from Dokital. The Ikkinni's right hand, fingers grasping the net ready for a cast, made a small gesture which the Terran could interpret neither as a welcome nor a refusal of aid, merely recognition.

Why he chose to stand with the native who by all evidence had left him helpless to face the same danger they were about to meet here, Kade could not have explained. Maybe it was that having been brought here by the stallion, manifestly eager for the coming fight, his warrior ancestors would not allow him any retreat.

The stallion halted, turned as the two men, to face the same curve of earth and stone. Now Kade could make out a barricade, a crosshatch of timber stakes. As that moved, the horse screamed such a vocal defiance as was echoed in ear-shattering sound from the walls of the bowl. Dokital crouched, the net coiled at his hampered feet. Kade, breathing faster, held his knife in readiness. With the three of them to face at once, one susti should be partly at a disadvantage.

The crude door was jerking upward, to display a dark hole, ragged enough about the edges to suggest a natural mountain cave. And the stench was now a choking wave of corruption, setting Kade to gagging.

How long would they have to wait? He remembered those dragging minutes back at the camp before the attack when he had been able to see his foe. Here at least, they knew the direction from which attack would come. Yet nothing save that overpowering odor had issued from the cave hole.

The drums, which had died to nothing since Kade's entrance, broke out in a wild beat. They must be stationed, the Terran thought, near the top of the amphitheater. The heavier roll on his left was balanced by a quick staccato tapping from the right. And that din would now drown out even the stallion's cries.

But the horse did not neigh, no longer tossed his head. He was as intent upon that hole as a feline might be at the hiding place of legitimate prey.

Maybe the beat of drum was acting as either an irritant or a summons. For the susti flashed out of hiding, not in the clumsy, wing-furled crawl with which its fellow had approached Kade, but in a leap which bore it into the air, wings beating.

For a startled second Kade believed the creature was more intent upon gaining the freedom of the night skies, than upon attacking its intended victim or victims. But if the susti was a captive, it was also trained in its role. For though that first flight carried it past the three in the arena, on to the throat of the gorge, it banked widely, its wings momentarily blotting out the streaming columns of firelight, to fly back.

The three were saved only by the pecularity of the enemy's hunting habits. Had it roved falconlike, pouncing on its prey from aloft, horse and men might have had little chance. But the susti had to kill such large opponents on the ground. So the glide of its return brought it down in a swoop as it headed for the horse. Perhaps it had fought with tethered Ikkinni sacrifices before and had the rudimentary intelligence to choose from the three the prey which appeared the easiest to subdue.

Only the stallion whirled with the agility of a veteran warrior and the susti missed its strike, while the hooves swung until one thudded against a leather wing, knocking the flyer off course. Those wings tried to beat, to raise the heavy body. Kade had to leap to avoid the sweep of one threshing surface.

Then the susti came to earth behind them, and horse and men turned to face the thoroughly enraged creature.

CHAPTER 11

DOKITAL'S NET LASHED OUT, in a cast to entangle the susti—he could not have managed such a feat alone—but to cut whip fashion across that pointed snout, flick punishment at the bulbous eyes. The thing squealed—the thin shriek partially drowned by the thunder of the drums and yet piercing enough to reach their ears through the din—gave way a step or two, an advantage the bound Ikkinni could not follow up.

But the stallion was not tied, nor was Kade. And now the Terran stooped, twisted the spear from Dokital's foothold before the native could stop him. With that in one hand and his knife in the other he circled to the right, trying to flank the creature.

And the horse, as if the animal caught a thought from the man, trotted back, came around to get behind the susti. One man against that horror would have had little chance, but the three who faced it now reduced the odds drastically.

Dokital lashed again, coming to the end of his ankle straps, striving to keep the susti occupied, occupied and grounded where they had the better of the battlefield. The beat of the drums reached a wild crescendo, deafening the men in the arena. Kade saw the stallion's open mouth, knew the horse was screaming, yet he could hear nothing of that equine rage. And the pounding beat was making him dizzy, attacking him with snaps of vertigo.

As yet the Terran saw no chance for a telling thrust against the susti. The creature used its wings as shields, holding him at a distance. And a spear's throw under one of those flapping barriers was beyond his skill. Kade watched for the opportunity to stab into some part of that obscene body, but the stallion went into action.

Using the same tactics followed before with such excellent results, the horse came up behind the susti and struck out, aiming for the hunched back of the creature. But, as if it had sensed that onslaught, the bat-thing clapped wings and those sharp-shoed weapons struck fruitlessly against leather edges, sliding off without harm. As the stallion went to his knees, Kade rushed in, the haft of the spear braced between arm and ribs—thrusting with all the strength of his body to ram the point home.

He felt the queer sensation of the head tearing into flesh and then a blow struck him, flattening him to the ground. Dazed, gasping for breath, he watched one of those hooked-wing claws curl over him, and brought up his knife hand in feeble defense.

The was no cutting edge on that improvised dagger, it had been made to stab. And somehow he held it point up against that wing paw as it beat down. The needle tip he had ground into being skewed between fine bones, the force of that blow drove his own hand back against his chest with crushing brutality. But the wing snapped up and Kade rolled free.

Dokital had enmeshed one wing and the darting head of the susti in the widest folds of his net, and was bent almost bow-shaped as he fought to hold fast. Kade got to the other side, caught the straining cords. In the firelight they could see the dance of the spear haft in the side of the threshing creature. But the wing which was free beat wildly, its wounded claw-paw grabbing for the two men.

The horse charged, head down, mouth wide open, using teeth against the hide of the thing's back, tearing loose both pelt and flesh. And in a second rush he used hooves once again, this time landing squarely on the chosen goal between the hunched shoulders.

So driven to the ground the susti pulled Kade with it, tore the net from Dokital's hold. However, for the men, the fight was over. Brought shoulder to shoulder by the susti's struggles they half supported each other as the stallion, with the lightning swift action of his kind, smashed the thing as he had smashed its fellow, days earlier. And handicapped by its wounds the Klorian terror was now an easy kill.

Kade became aware that the clamor of the drums was dying, as if those drummers masked in the high shadows on the arena slopes were so bemused by the action below that they were dropping out of the infernal chorus which had summoned the susti. Now the Terran could detect individual beats in the once solid wave of noise, the rhythm was irregular as well as dying.

Yet no one had come from those serried ranks of watchers to interfere in the fight. Would a successful kill of the captive devil allow the three their freedom, or merely delay the vengeance of the watching natives? Judging by their treatment of Dokital they were hostile—

The susti was finished, a pulp beneath the dancing hooves of the horse. Kade pushed away from Dokital, circled about the mass on the ground to near the snorting, still wild-eyed four-footed fighter. He called softly, held out his hands.

For a second or two he was afraid that the animal was too excited to hear him. Then the head turned, the eyes regarded the Terran. Placing one foot carefully before the other as if he walked on some treacherous surface, the stallion came to Kade. That proud head was lowered until the forelock brushed against the man's bare chest, and the Terran's hands smoothed up the arch of the sweating neck, fondled the ears. Without hackmore he had no rider's control, yet this was a time to impress the native watchers and Kade must take it. Still caressing the horse, he mounted.

The stallion neighed, to be heard above the almost dead rattle of the few remaining drums. Kade, one hand on the stiff mane where the neck arch arose from the body, his other up, palm out and before him, dared to call out in the speech of the Trade post:

"Ho! Here are warriors!"

The last drum was dead. He could believe that he heard a sigh of concentrated breathing along those rows of spectators who were only a blur beyond the reaches of the firelight.

"Here are warriors!" He kneed the stallion, kept his seat as the horse obeyed with a high stepping prance of forefeet. And from the right he heard Dokital echo the boast.

"Here are the warriors!"

By all that he knew of Ikkinni custom, those in the darkness must acknowledge that cry and admit equality with the victors or send forth a champion to dispute a claim which was a dare to every fighting man in that half-seen assemblage. And what he would do if such a champion appeared, Kade had no idea. But among his own kind bravery and skill in battle were recognized passports to diplomatic relations, even between old enemies. And so it might prove in this other culture solar systems away.

"It is Dokital of the line of Dok the long-armed, of Amsog of the quick wit, of Gid of the red spear. It is Kade of the starwalkers from the far skies. It is Swiftfeet of the horse kind." Dokital threw the words at the still silent throng.

"Here are warriors who have fought the devil kind, the devil kind of the collars, the devil kind who obey those of the collars, the devil kind of the stony places." Dokital jerked the end of net. The crushed head of the susti rolled in gruesome answer, and the stallion pawed the earth, danced a step closer to his trampled foe.

"Here are warriors!" For the third time the Ikkinni flung that into the faces of the massed tribesmen.

The crackle of the flames cut the night and below that small sound Kade thought he could detect another murmur, as the whisper of a breeze running along the slopes of the arena. They waited.

Then, from directly above the cave door of the susti, there was a stir in the shadows, a ripple of figures rising, giving place to a small group of natives who stepped out in the full light of the fires. They halted there, five of them, well built men with the glint of jewelry on their upper arms, their belts, but no telltale rings about their throats. And, as the three from the plains faced them, each raised his spear and drove it point deep in the sand, ceremoniously disarming themselves.

"Here are warriors—"

Kade relaxed. Dokital dropped his net. The stallion stood as a statue.

"It is Kakgil of the line of Akil of the stone arm."

"It is Dartig of the line of Tigri the wind-swift."

"It is Farqui of the Inner Cliffs."

"It is Losigil of the Bitter Water Place."

"It is Vuqic of the line of Stigi the strong heart."

Each announced himself in turn. Their names, their identifications meant nothing to Kade, but he memorized them, sure that none of these men were petty chieftains with only a handful of followers. Their pride of bearing rather argued that he was fronting what might be the tribal leaders of the free interior, men on whom the Styor might have set fabulous prices. And if that were so, and he could make peaceful contact—Kade fought down his own soaring excitement, this was no time to hope for too much, to grow careless.

He who had named himself Kakgil made a quick downwards sweep with one hand. The cords holding Dokital twitched, loosened. With a kick the Ikkinni drew one foot out of an imprisoning circle, and then the other. The ex-slave stepped forward, leaving his bonds on the sand behind him.

"It greets Kakgil, as one who runs the high places to one who holds the spear over them."

"It greets the runner." Kakgil responded gravely. He plucked his spear out of the sand, reversed it with a graceful toss, and held out the butt to Dokital. The other took the weapon, spun it in a like fashion and drove the point into the ground again before his own feet. Kade guessed at the symbolism behind that action. If these two had been enemies, that enmity was now at an end.

"It has spoken true words," Dokital continued, and now there was again a hint of challenge in his tone. He put up one hand, drew his fingers lightly along the curve of the stallion's neck. The horse turned his head, regarded the Ikkinni, but accepted the attention with the same docility with which had had allowed Kade to mount.

"This is Swiftfeet, and the kind of Swiftfeet are for warriors, even as it said."

Kakgil looked at the Ikkinni, the horse and the Terran.

"It has spoken true words," he acknowledged. "The evil tale came to us out of the night, now we know that is evil. Swiftfeet is the friend of those in the heights. This is so!" His voice arose, carrying authority, the determination of his will, and again the murmur whispered about the arena. One by one the other chieftains echoed him. And so Kade found they had not only won the fight, but also acceptance among the free peoples of the hidden mountain valleys.

Before the dawn Kade, the horses, and Dokital were taken to one of those well concealed villages and the Terran witnessed for the first time the life of the Ikkinni who were not linked to the Styor will by the collars.

The architects of that village had taken advantage of a natural feature of the mountain side in their planning of what was in effect one great house set cunningly into a vast half-cavern where the overhang of rock not only provided the erection of stone and fire-dried clay with added protection, but effectively concealed it from any but ground level detection.

"Once warriors lived in skin tents," Kakgil noted the Terran's interest. "For then hunters followed the kwitu. Afterwards there were hunters for hunters, and those who wandered away from the high places could be easily netted and taken. Thus we make these hidden places."

Kade studied the rough walls, the small, easily defended entrances, and smaller, high window holes. The structure was undeniably crude, put together by those who had worked only with a general idea of what they must accomplish and primitive, untaught skills. Compared to Cor, Kakgil's village was a child's sand castle set against a finely finished plasta playhouse. Yet it represented a vast, awesome step forward into another kind of civilization, made in only a generation or two by men who had been roving hunters. And the potential it suggested was startling.

"This is a fine place!" The Terran gave hearty tribute not only to the city-house but to the labor and the dream which had brought it into being. And his sincerity was plain to the chieftain, for Kakgil gave a small sound, close to a human chuckle.

"To us a fine place," he agreed. "There are others," he waved a hand to the spreading peaks of the mountains. "Many others."

Kade discovered that there had been no great consolidation among the free Ikkinni. They still lived in bands of a few family clans, and such a village as he was shown harbored no more than a hundred natives at the most. But several such were linked by loose alliance, and the gathering in the arena had been comprised of the adults of five such communities.

The Terran established a camp with the horses outside the cave of the village and he was not surprised when Dokital chose to remain with him. They were eating cakes of ground grass seeds supplied them by their hosts when Kade asked his first question.

115

"It was left tied . . . for the susti—"

Dokital swallowed, perhaps to gain time. But he did not evade a reply.

"Tied, yes; for susti, no."

"Why?"

"It was not friend. The starwalker knew secret to free Ikkinni but would not help. It was made safe."

Kade could follow that line of reasoning.

"So it was left while Dokital went for the free warriors?"

"That is so. It has said those are for warriors." He pointed to the horses.

"So Dokital took the horses to impress the free men, but they would not believe, holding the stranger prisoner?"

"That is so. It was struck from the back of the runner by a net. It was out of its body for a time. When it returned there were bonds, and it was judged a thing of the collar masters sent to bring monsters into the hills where the masters can not come on their flying things."

"But how did this tale of monsters spread so far from the flat lands?" Kade asked.

Dokital's lips shaped a half-smile. "Ask of the mountains where blows the force of the wind-breath. Drums talk among the hills, men tell false tales to those who have not seen with their two eyes, heard with their own ears, touched with the fingers of their hands. The collar masters spoke and the ripple of their speaking reached far."

Kade began to understand the pattern. The Styor had tried to make sure not only of the Traders at the post, but of any who might possibly escape into the mountains. The aliens had planted this story of monsters, seen that the rumor trickled back by "bush telegraph" into the holds of the out-laws, thereby making sure of a hostile reception for any re-fugees.

"Now warriors believe differently?"

Dokital selected another cake. "The warriors of five tribes have seen with their own eyes, heard with their lips. Soon they will come to this fire, ask for more talk concerning Swift-feet and his wife ones."

But it was not about horses that the two Ikkinni who stepped quietly into the camp came to talk. Kakgil and the taller, thinner native who had introduced himself in the arena as Vuqic, stood waiting until Kade arose. And then, using the same ceremony as they had before, they pushed spear points into the earth.

"There is fire, and food," the Terran recited the formula he had learned at the post. "It is welcome," he inclined his head toward Kakgil and Vuqic, remaining on his feet until both were seated.

Kakgil came to the point brusquely. "There is a story that the one from beyond the stars has a new weapon to make collars into nothingness."

"Part of such a story is the truth," Kade admitted. "But there is this also; that when the weapon makes nothingness of the collars, some of those wearing them die."

"That is the truth," Dokital added. "Yet it is free." His hand went to his throat, rubbing the caloused skin where a collar had once chaffed.

"These weapons which make a collar nothing. Let us see one."

Kade held up empty hands. "One each of those did the starwalkers carry. It's is gone blasted away, and so are the rest. For the masters of the collars brought the fire death to all my clan."

"So has that story been told also," Kakgil assented. "But if these weapons exist beyond the stars, then those who fly into the far sky can bring us more. Do they not give the masters many things in exchange for the skins of musti? And we know caves in which musti have never been troubled. We can build a mountain of skins in return for such weapons."

"There is this," Kade brought his own problem to the fore. "A ship of the starwalkers came two suns ago to the burnt place where its clan lived. When those in that ship find no

117

life, they will depart again. Maybe to come no more. And already that ship may have returned to the stars."

"In the high places there are drums to send thoughts and calls from one clan holding to the next." Vuqic spoke for the first time. "Have the starwalkers no drums to sound among the star?"

"There is a chance that there is one. But between this place and that lies much ground, also many hunting parties of collared ones. Out in the open country the flying ships of the collar masters can capture or kill those who try to reach the burned place. And it can not be sure that the drum is still there."

Kakgil laid a stick upon the small fire. "This matter shall be thought upon," he declared. "Now what of this Swiftfeet who serves warriors without a collar? Why was it brought?"

Kade noted that the Ikkinni gave the horse the "it" designation of a man, rather than the "that" of an animal.

"There is a saying," Vuqic cut in once more, "that it was to be taken to a master of collars—the high master—for a new toy thing."

"So was the thought," Kade said cautiously.

"But not all the thought," Dokital corrected. "It," he indicated Kade, "said that the runners are for warriors. And what master of collars is a true warrior? Kill is the order, but there is no spear in the hand of such a one. A warrior kills for himself, not afar and by word only."

Kade relied on what he knew of Ikkinni customs. "There is a story—in truth a story," he used their own idiomatic approach of one of the honored elders of their kind, a born story teller whose phenomenal memory and powers of invention could recall one of their age-old sagas, or add a new tale fashioned out of the events of the latest clan hunt. And to the Terran's gratification he saw that they were giving him close attention.

"Where it dwells among the stars there were once those who were also in their way masters of collars. And these same

animals were ridden into battle by their warriors, so that the
other peoples who had no such helpers could be easily hunted
for killing or caught to be made into collared ones. But the
animals were new to the land which they found a good
one, and they broke free from their masters, running into
hidden places. And the Ikkinni of that land found the beasts
were also friends to them, so they stole more from the city
places of the masters." He simplified, made into a story they
could understand the explosion of history which had marked
the coming of the horse to his own plains-roaming race, and
what had occured thereafter. And seeing their gleaming eyes,
Kade knew that the parallel was plain to them.

Dokital spoke first. "These are a treasure to keep!"

"Ha, so!" agreed Kakgil. "But that is locked in time. Now
is now and there is the weapon of the starwalkers. Give such
into the hands of warriors and no hunters or collar masters
shall enter these lands!"

"The weapons are beyond the stars!" Kade objected, afraid
they would demand which he could not possibly give them.

"Other things have come from the stars. This is a thing to
be thought on." Kakgil arose, reached for his spear. "This star
drum for your signaling must be thought on, too."

CHAPTER 12

THIS TIME THE TERRAN headed toward the plains by night
instead of day, and he did not go alone. A picked band of
Ikkinni trackers, seasoned to the alarms and cautions of the
hunted, went as guides, and, he suspected, guards. The
natives were determined not to lose the off-worlder until they
had made some sort of a bargain for stunners. Although Kade
had continued to argue that the Trade ship might have long
since left Klor.

119

The very slim chance of using the hidden com was one he did not like to consider. He could not push out of mind the doubt that he might now be an exile on the alien planet, without hope of rescue. So he tried to concentrate on the business of getting safely back to the destroyed post.

They threaded a more complicated route than the one he had used days earlier, once skirting a camp of collared men, sleeping feet to the fire, their Overman sheltered in a leanto of branches. Kade's Ikkinni neighbor toyed with his spear as he eyed them thoughtfully. But any miss from a death stroke meant torture for the slaves and the native did not use his weapon.

"Two watchers," he whispered to Kade, his motion only dimly to be seen in the light of the dying fire as he motioned right and left.

The Terran could detect no sound except the usual ones of the night. A sleeping slave stirred, and both watchers tensed. Kade had a knife, a spear under his hand. But he longed for a stunner. The slave muttered and rolled over, but his restlessness did not arouse any of his fellows.

With finger pressure on the Terran's shoulder, the Ikkinni signaled Kade to the right. And the off-worlder applied all his knowledge of woodcraft to melt into the brush as noiselessly as possible. Together they flitted into a small gully where another joined them.

"It on watch now sleeps?"

The low voice of Kakgil answered. "It does."

Again their party drew together and pushed on. False dawn found them in file along the banks of a stream where rank, reedlike grass grew. The Ikkinni put the natural features of the spreading bog to their use. Mud, grey-green, was scraped from holes, plastered to the haired skins, to Kade's breeches, chest and shoulders. Handfuls of dried grass laid into that sticky coating so that every man could fade undetected into the landscape.

They continued to stick to the bog, following a trail, the

markers of which Kade could not discover. Perhaps they existed only in the memory of the native who now led. As far as the Terran could determine they were now to the north of the former post, well out into the plains region.

Looming up now and again were islands of firmer land on which they paused to rest. And, as the first lines of the climbing sun split the sky, they ate grain cakes, drank sparingly from the leather bottle Kakgil carried. It contained a thin, acid liquid which burned the tongue, but satisfied the body's desire for water.

The village chieftain smoothed out a stretch of clay, marked on it with a stick. A finger's whirl was the swamp about them, a dot the site of the post. Kade began to realize that, far from being kept to the mountains as the Styor had contended and the Traders believed, these free natives must have made countless scouting trips into the plains in which their fathers had been hunted, each carrying in a trained memory vast knowledge of the lost lands. What raiders they would make, given adequate weapons and the means for swift movement!

But this was not a matter of future guerrilla attacks against Styor holdings. It was their own safe visit to a site which could easily be patrolled from both air and ground level. The Terran digested that crude map, tried to align it with his memories of the countryside.

If the scout ship had been sighted by the Styor—and unless the aliens were possessed by a suicidal folly they would have left a sentry near the post—there could be a Klorian force at hand already, or on their way to the burnoff. Kade warned of that and found that Kakgil had accepted such a possible peril. If the Styor were at the site, the mountaineers would leave a scout in hiding and withdraw, to try again. And the Terran understood the monumental patience of these people who had fought for a century against drastic odds. The drive which had sent his own species into the star lanes met time as an enemy, these men used it as a tool.

The sun which had promised so brightly in the dawn hours,

shone only for a space. Clouds gathered above the mountains. Dokital, pointing to the wall of mist hanging above their back trail, laughed.

"The Planner has planned, now the Spearman readies His weapon. This is a good day, a good thing, a good plan."

Wind rasped across the plains, struck chill, lifting the vapors of the bog, thrusting at the tangled covering of their island. The signs of the storm suggested one more severe than any Kade had witnessed on Klor.

With the push of the wind at their backs they obeyed Kakgil's order to move on. Half an hour later, cloaked in the deepening murk, they splashed from a shallow runnel of water onto a solid strip of earth marking the fringe of the plains.

A Styor flyer might just try to buck the wind, but Kade doubted it unless the pilot had definite orders to operate. This weather should ground all routine patrols. But the method of advance, in a zig-zag pattern with frequent halts to take cover, proved to the Terran that Kakgil did not intend to underestimate the enemy.

Lightning crisped in the sky, bringing the tingling smell of ozone. Another such flash halted them, half blinded, and Kade was sure that unleashed energy had struck not too far away. Could the burn-off scar, by some weird chemistry of the glassy slag, be drawing the electrical fury of the storm?

That whip of flashing death was merely the forerunner of rain. Rain and wind which beat, pummeled their bodies, washing away their mud disguises, leaving them gasping in a blanket of rushing water. They tied their weapons to their belts and linked hands, to stagger on, backs bent to the storm. The falling fury of the water, the dark of the clouds which held it, concealed from Kade whether the Trade ship still stood, fins planted on the landing apron.

The off-worlder stumbled and went to his knees, losing his hold on Dokital, his line partner. His palm came down on slick, wet surface, smooth yet rippling. What he had fallen over was the edge of the burn site. And there was no waiting ship.

They could not walk across that surface crust, running wet and too slippery for feet shod in either Terran boots or the hide coverings of the Ikkinni. On hands and knees the party crept over the glassy expanse, searching for the opening to the underground installation.

Kade found it difficult to connect this slick slab of crystallized earth and stone with the square of buildings, the inner courtyard, he had known. He could not even guess from what quarter of the compass he had approached the scar. Where their goal might now lie could be within inches, feet, yards, or the length of the scar.

It was not the Terran who located the break in the crust. Kade, alerted by the message running from man to man along the advancing Ikkinni, came to the pit he had to explore by touch rather than sight. One or two of the Team *had* refuged below, to be freed by the ship's crew. Whether the com was still there and undestroyed he must learn.

Water poured over his fingers, cascaded into the depths. That flood could ruin the com in a short time. Kade managed to make the Ikkinni understand what had to be done. One of the hunting nets was slung over the edge and Kade used it for a ladder. As he descended water rose about his feet, lapped at his calves, wet the breeches above the tops of his boots. Then his feet met solid surface, he could feel walls on either side but not ahead.

The passage, if passage it was, ran on. And the water, pouring from above, was rising. If that unknown path ahead took a downward way perhaps the flood had already sealed it.

Kade shivered. If the water reached the com he was exiled. Time was not on his side now. He released his hold on the net, waded forward, waves washing about him, splashing to mid-thigh.

The footing was good, although the flood hindered swift movement. He kept one hand on the wall as a guide. And when he had gone some twenty paces he knew that the water was not rising any more swiftly than it had in the entrance pit.

On his twenty-first step the black dark of the pocket was lost in a flick of light. Over his wet head shown the green glow of an atmo lamp. He must have crossed some automatic signal set in the wall. Ahead were two more such lights, their round balls reflected from the curling waves through which he labored. Three lights then a sealed door, a door with a locking hand hollow in its center panel.

Was that lock tuned to open to the flesh pattern of any Terran, or only to certain members of the Team? But who could select survivors in advance?

Kade wiped his right hand back and forth across his chest, tucked it into his armpit for a long moment, hoping to rid it of the chill moisture. Then he fitted fingers and palm into the mould and waited. The slow creep of water was now washing a fraction of an inch higher every time it slapped against his body.

There was no warning click. Kade snatched his hand away as the panel flipped back into the wall. Around him the water rushed on, lapping into the room, swirling around the few pieces of furniture. There were wall bunks, some open ration tins on a pull-down table, signs of hasty leaving.

But what Kade wanted was still there; the com. He splashed to that shelf. However as he reached for the starting button he saw another object, poised directly before the communicator. And he had been briefed in the proper use of that sectional rod mounted on a firm base.

Now he knew that the men who had waited in that room, or some member of the ship's crew, had suspected—or hoped —for his escape. There would be no answer to any message sent from the com. Perhaps the installation itself had been booby-trapped to prevent examination by native or Styor— but he did not need it.

Kade caught up that tube. Sealed into it were delicate works, the technology of which was beyond him. But it would work when and if he desired. Cradling it against him, the Terran made his way back along the waterlogged passage. He had only to locate a proper site, set up what he carried, and there would be a new landing field on Klor, one not supervised by the Styor.

"It has?" Kakgil pushed close as he climbed out of the pit.

"It has a Star drum!" Kade fended off the other's hand. "But only it can sound this drum."

"Sound then!" Dokital moved in from the other side.

Kade shook his head. "Not here. Not now. A safer place, in the mountains."

With what he carried he wanted to be as far from the post as he could get before the storm ceased to protect them from the threat of Styor sky sweeps. And he conveyed that urgency to the Ikkinni.

The rainfall lessened as they plodded on, their pace which had begun as a trot, dropping to a dogged walk. Towards sunset they gained refuge in a criss-cross maze of foothills and they camped wet and cold that night, not daring a fire.

Two days later they came again into the valley of Kakgil's village to find it deserted. Only the horses, still free, welcomed Kade. He mounted volunteers from his escort, Kakgil one of them, and they headed on, into the heart of the range where the most daring slave hunters had never ventured.

A full week of the longer Klorian days passed before their small party caught up with an Ikkinni war party. Kakgil called a conference of scouts who knew the land while Kade set up his signal tube in demonstration, explained the terrain needed and why. Hunters compared notes, grew heated in dispute, finally agreed and voiced their suggestion through Iskug, who had joined the band.

"Two suns, two sleeps away, there is a place where long ago the Spearman struck deep into the earth." He rounded his hands into a cup. "It has seen the ships from the stars. If it who drives such a ship is skillful, the ship could be set into this place as so." He inserted a finger tip into the curled fingers of his other hand.

"This is the only place?" Iskug's description was too graphic to be reassuring. The Ikkinni agreed that the described crater was the best and safest landing the range had to offer.

Later Kade, standing at the end of a grueling climb and looking down into that hole, was not sure. There was floor space enough, yes, to set a scout down. And the surface appeared as level as any ground. But the fitting of the ship into the hollow required skill such as only a veteran pilot would possess. However Trade pilots were top men.

They made their way to the floor of the crater. The eruption which had caused the blowout must have been a cataclysmic one. Kade held the signal at shoulder level, triggered a thumb button, and slowly turned, giving the hidden lens the complete picture of this rock-walled well for broadcasting. Then he walked to what he judged was the center of the open space and secured the tube on the ground with latching earth spikes. Last of all he brought his hand down sharply on the pointed tip of the cone. There was no way for him to know whether the broadcaster was really working, his answer could only come, in time, from off-world.

Kade sat outside the crude hut at the lip of the crater. His calendar was a series of scratches on the boulder which served as a section of wall. By that reckoning he had been doing sentry duty here more than a month.

His thoughts were series of *ifs* now. *If* the signal, lonely in the crater, had somehow been damaged during their journey here, then the broadcaster had never been beamed starward at all.

If the Ikkinni lost patience they might turn on him. Styor parties were raiding unceasingly into the lower valleys driving many clans from their villages. The spring hunting was interrupted. Hunger stalked the refugees. Let some chieftain pin the blame on the presense of the off-world fugitive and Kade might be delivered to the aliens for a truce.

If the Styor continued to bore in they would force his own withdrawal from here.

If—if—if—

A whistle from below broke his moody thoughts. Dokital, his dark-haired body hardly distinguishable from the rocks until he moved, came up at a pace suggesting trouble.

"Slavers!" The Ikkinni reported curtly.

"Where?"

"The water valley. They make camp."

Never before had any Styor-controlled party come this close to the crater. And if the aliens were establishing a camp this early in the day, they meant a stay of more than one night's duration.

"Kakgil—the horses?"

"They move north taking the kwitu trail."

That was a slight lifting of the Terran's burden of responsibility. Kakgil would move his people and the off-world animals they now cherished to safety, putting a stretch of rough and easily defended country between themselves and the invaders.

"It goes?" Dokital fidgeted by the hut. Having once worn a collar he was not minded to be trapped again.

"It must stay for awhile." Within the hour, before sunset, at any moment, the Terran ship could land. He must remain here. "Let Dokital go."

"Not so." The Ikkinni sat down, laid his spear across his knee. "From this place the evil ones can be seen, they can not creep up as if they net the musti."

Maybe they could not bring a net, Kade thought grimly, but the aliens had other and more potent ways of bringing the hunted to terms. And he was sure that the Styor had provided these servants with them.

Once they sighted a group of collar slaves searching for fire wood. But there was no indication that their own perch was under suspicion. In the hut they had water, two day's rations of seed cakes. And they could stretch that supply if need be.

"One comes."

"Whereso?"

"By the rock of the kwitu horn."

Kade followed the line of Dokital's pointing spear tip. The newcomer was no Ikkinni, collared or free, nor the Overman of a squad. Away from a carrying-chair, the other marks of his Klorian godship, a Styor was climbing stiffly up the rugged slope. He held one arm bent at chest level and divided his attention between his footing and a band about his wrist. In his other hand he carried the ultimate in the aliens' armament —the needler!

Flight was cut off. The Terran judged that the wristband was some kind of tracking device, perhaps centered on his own thought waves. He could walk backward, step out into the space of the crater, and crash down to end near the signal. Only then the Styor might use that signal for bait.

On the other hand, suppose he was needled down. Would the alien pass the signal unnoticed? The Styor was astute enough to investigate why the off-worlder had camped here. Either way the bejeweled, slim humanoid had all the cards on his side. Kade had overestimated the sloth of the pampered lords, underestimated their desire to make sure of the last Terran.

About the Styor's middle was a anti-person belt. No overlord would risk his precious skin with the slightest chance of a counterattack. The spear in Kade's hold, any Ikkinni net, a rock thrown by a desperate man, would rebound from the aura now about the alien as from a dura-steel wall.

Unless—Kade searched the ground about him for some suggestion of offence or defense. The Styor could probably track them if they tried to run for it. He did not know the range of the instrument the alien wore. On the other hand he was not going to be needled down without some counterattack, no matter how feeble.

More to gain time than by any plan the Terran signalled Dokital away from the hut, along the edge of the crater. The rough terrain hid them from actual sighting by the Styor, though his locator would bring him on their track.

Single file the two walked a narrow line along the drop. An idea grew in Kade's mind. A chance he was now desperate enough to try.

The Styor reached the hut, did not even glance into its empty interior, but came on, treading the same way the fugitives had taken. Again Kade signed to Dokital, sending the Ikkinni away from him. Then the Terran halted, balancing his spear in his hand. A few feet beyond, the ancient bowl of the crater was split with a crack wide enough to offer protection to a slender Terran body. He marked that down.

He was waiting as the Styor's head arose, the alien's eyes raised from the device on his wrist to the man before him. Then Kade hurled his spear.

The aim was true, though the point struck that invisible guard a good six inches away from the Styor's chest. And the involuntary reaction of the other carried through even as Kade had hoped. A flinch backward set the alien's booted heel on a patch of smooth stone. There was a wide flail of arms as the Styor went backward into thin air.

His safety belt would save his life, but now he would have the inner wall of the crater to climb. The Terran's attack had bought them a measure of time. Kade sped to the crevice, Dokital joining him. The Styor was floating down, settling to the floor of the crater. But they had only gained a few moments of time, no real escape. Only—

Kade's arm went about Dokital, he carried the native with him in a rush as from overhead came a clap of sound louder than any thunder. Stone scraped skin raw as they tumbled into the rock crack. Above there was a flare of blinding light, and Kade hid his eyes with one bruised arm. The roar of a ship's tail flames as it braked into the heart of the crater was deafening.

Perhaps the Styor had had one instant of horror, a second's realization of descending death—then nothing at all. The same end he or his fellows had visited on the Trade post had already been his.

As the Terran and the Ikkinni crawled from their refuge the fumes of molten sand arose from that cup. Set neatly in the center was the star-ship. Kade climbed to the rim of the rock wall, waved at that expanse of pitted metal although no hatch had yet opened. But the response came soon enough, a ramp swung out to ground against the mountain some feet below him. He slid down, hearing his boots clang against its surface, hardly yet able to believe in that opportune arrival.

Somehow he was not surprised to be met by Abu in the cabin adjoining the control section. Nor was he more than mildly interested in the fact that the Commander's companion there wore five ticks of gold on the collar of his tunic.

"That's about it, sir." He had cut his report to the pertinent facts as best he could. Reaction was beginning to undermine the exultant self-confidence which had accompanied him into that cabin. There was a black list of sins of omission and commission which could be charged against him. What had Ristoff said on Lodi? If he fouled this last chance— And now the Book-of-Rules boys could pick Kade Whitehawk into little bits.

"Most reprehensible!" The five tick VIP pressed the button to turn off his recorder. "Now," the officer pushed away the machine with a gesture of repudiation. "Let us consider our real business."

"Most satisfactory." Abu's tone mimicked that used only moments before, but the words were different.

Somehow the formality of their meeting was gone as if the VIP had skinned off a tight tunic. He grinned and punched refreshment keys in the tabletop.

"A nice piece of work, one to keep rolling, Whitehawk."

"Roll right along," Abu joined the approbation. "Harder to stop now than a meteor with a musti net."

Kade was almost brave enough to demand an explanation.

"The time has come, sir," Abu added, "to initiate another fledgling into the fold."

Kade accepted the drink bubble the VIP extended, sucked a full mouthful of *Stardew*, Mars-side proof, without knowing just what he swallowed.

"Yes, a tale to unfold." The VIP drank. He bore, Kade decided critically, a not too distant resemblance to Che'in at that Trader's blandest and most irritating.

"The answer to your leading question," the officer continued blandly," is that you've passed a little test with all jets flaming. You were handpicked for a job, sent here to use your wits. And you did. You see, there is the Policy—and the Plan."

"Seldom do the twain meet," Abu intoned piously.

His superior chuckled. "Be glad, Commander, that the right hand and the left do not shake too often. This is the way of it, young man. We have our loyal servants of Trade, who live and breathe by the Book, never, never make a mistake, and are a shining glory to the Service. Then we have some blacksheep who also serve in their rebellious fashion. We call them the warrior breed." He paused, sucked at his drink bubble. "Their first general testing is to be sent to a planet where the Styor are really unbearable. If they can scrape through an 'incident' without being too far damned by the resultant publicity, then they are promoted to a Team on such a world as Klor.

"As you know, each Team is selected from widely different basic Terran racial stocks with a few of the normal "Trade-type" for cover. It is always our hope that one of our under-cover 'warriors' will find inspiration in his new enviroment and manage to pull off a coup which will give another nudge toward the upsetting of Styor power. A pinch here, a prod there, little irritations breaking out all over the galaxy, yet nothing they can actually connect with us or any plan. That is *the* Plan!"

Kade saw. It was looking at a familiar landscape from an angle so bizarre he might indeed be viewing a new world.

131

"But the Styor burnt the post. Why?"

"There is such a thing as coincidence. Here your bit of pushing worked into the High-Lord-Pac's own bid for fame and fortune. *He* is trying out a formula for getting rid of unwelcome Terrans and building up a reputation for law enforcement at one and the same time. We'll let him think he got away with it—for awhile. Long enough for your experiment to get a good start. What have you in mind for these Ikkinni? Mounted raids and guerrilla warfare?"

Kade nodded. He had a feeling that the VIP was far ahead of him, that his one or two bright discoveries were a matter of kindergarten games in an obscure backyard playground.

"He might be persuaded to see it through," Abu remarked. "That's the third step in our real Service, Whitehawk."

"Five horses—and the mountains crawling with Styor. How many years do you think it would take to make Cor uneasy?" Kade roused himself to demand.

"Oh, you don't have to have it quite as rugged as all that." The VIP clicked open a wall storage compartment, brought forth a belt and holstered stunner. He drew the weapon, slid it across the table to Kade's hand.

"Now that is something you will find useful. We've pushed through a rush order at the base, and can let you have about fifty now, with a drop of more to arrange for later. Try that on a collar control and you'll see some pleasing results, without obnoxious side features. Horses—Well, another drop of those will take some doing. But clear us a plains-side place and we'll oblige. That is, of course, if you stay on here."

Kade fingered the stunner. He did not in the least doubt that it would act just as promised. Fifty of those to hand—why, they could free the slave packs now hunting them here, use the knowledge of the freed men against their masters—Open a section of plain—Yes, it could be done. A raid in the outer fringe, a landing site far enough from Cor that they could keep it open for two Klorian days, maybe longer. He heard Abu laugh.

"The relay is clicking, sir. Already he marches to unmask the High-Lord-Pac."

Kade grinned. "Not quite as fast as all that, sir."

The VIP nodded. "Start small, and don't push too hard. This may be *your* big war, it's only a small skirmish in the Plan."

Kade buckled on the stunner belt. "Tell me, sir, how long has the Plan been in operation."

For the first time since he clicked off the recorder the officer lost his genial air of satisfaction. "For about two hundred years."

Kade stared. "And how long—"

"Until," Abu answered softly, "a push here, a push there topples a star empire. An event I am beginning to doubt any of us here will live to see. Not that that matters."

And, thought Kade, perhaps it did not. But one could get a lot of satisfaction out a good stiff push—with the Styor on the receiving end.

ANDRE NORTON

A Profile by Lin Carter

For at least three reasons, Andre Norton is something of a phenomenon in science fiction today. Ostensibly a juvenile author, she happens also to be very popular with adult readers. A full-time science fiction professional, she is *never* published in the magazines. And—despite her undeniable gift for colorful prose, exciting narrative that is entertaining and told with verve and gusto, not to mention the consistently high level of imaginative invention that runs throughout her work—she is largely ignored by "serious" reviewers, and, when discussed at all, usually underrated. I mention these somewhat puzzling factors in her career without attempting to explain them. Nevertheless, they do tend to render her unique among modern science fiction writers and worthy of this inquiry.

She is also extraordinarily prolific. In fact, by the end of 1966 she had published over fifty-two books.

Her real name, no great secret, of course, is Alice Mary Norton. She was born about fifty years ago in Cleveland and has spent most of her life there. Her first love seems to have been, appropriately enough, science fiction. And, although she has written stories of many different moods and manners—pirate yarns, a murder mystery, fairy-tale romances, Civil War stories, children's fantasies, Westerns, and straight adult fantasies—well over half of her work to date has been devoted to our field.

She has told me she encountered Edgar Rice Burroughs and Ray Cummings at an early age, and decided almost on the spot that she wanted to write in their style . . . which, in a way, she does. Like their novels, her books are fast-moving fantastic romances dealing with the primary emotions, easily comprehensible by the teen-age readers. She tells me: "My first book—which was later rewritten and appeared as my second (*i.e.*, RALESTONE LUCK, Appleton Century, 1938)—was written in high school and my first book was published before I was out of my teens."

This may help to explain the sympathy between her work and her (predominately) juvenile audience. She has also been a children's librarian in Cleveland, which was probably a factor in her decision to publish primarily for the older kids. At any rate, when Miss Norton entered the field of juvenile science fiction, the market—what little there was, and there wasn't much —was largely the unchallenged domain of writers of what you might call limited powers. I am refering to the Carl H. Claudys and Roy Rockwoods and Victor Appletons. There just was no precedent for inventive, truly imaginative juvenile science fiction of adult calibre when she began publishing. Things stayed about at the Claudy-Rockwood-Appleton level of maturity until Robert Heinlein busted in and showed publishers, editors, and reviewers that you could *too* write good, solid, intelligent science fiction for kids.

52 BOOKS IN 32 YEARS

Andre Norton's first book, THE PRINCE COMMANDS, was straight adventure rather than science fiction. Appleton brought it out in 1934. The first eight of her books came slowly, paced out over fifteen years. Among those was HUON OF THE HORN (Harcourt, Brace, 1948), a luminous, graceful retelling of the Old French *chanson de geste* about Huon de Bordeaux, a Carolingian fantasy laid in the days after Roland and Oliver got theirs in the Pyrenees. Young Huon zips about from Hither to Thither (in the approved style of the classical *chanson*), accepts a dare to pull out the beard of the King of Babylon, makes off with his daughter, meets Shakespeare's Oberon and eventually succeeds to the Throne of All Faerie when the Elf-King abdicates to spend an eternity-long vacation in Paradise, which seems to have been pictured by the Old French Romancers as a sort of Riviera of its day. It's a jolly good yarn, and I'm happy Ace Books brought it to our attention.

I suppose these first eight books helped mould Andre Norton's style. They certainly established her as a reliable producer of action yarns, and gave her a good publisher she was to continue to use for nearly twenty years.

Her first science fiction novel was STAR MAN'S SON (Harcourt, Brace, 1952), quickly paperbacked by Ace Books, under the title of DAYBREAK—2250 A.D. This paperback edition was doubtless a rather risky experiment on the part of Ace, for it must have been among the first juveniles between soft covers. But the fans liked it, reviewers were kind, and it sold like crazy. It was one of those experiments that paid off. Today, of all the authors Ace publishes (including most of the top writers in science fiction's history, from Burroughs and E. E. Smith, Heinlein and Van Vogt, on to Jack Vance and Henry Kuttner and Avram Davidson), Miss Norton is the top best-seller of them all.

After the success of this book, Miss Norton had some confidence in her favorite medium and her production began to pick up rapidly. From then to right now, she has averaged about three books a year—often enough, four—and this is as good as Burroughs was doing in the prime of his enormous popularity.

For a sample of the variety in subject and form that are typical of Andre Norton, let's pick an average year, 1954. She had four new books on the market that year. The first one, AT SWORD'S POINT, from Harcourt, was a juvenile historical and a real rouser. The second, from her "alternate" publisher, World Publishing Company, was a science fiction anthology called SPACE PIONEERS. Number three, from Hammond, was her one and only mystery, MURDERS FOR SALE. And the fourth, also under the World imprint, was THE STARS ARE OURS, a science fiction novel, now an Ace paperback.

OPENING UP BRAND NEW MARKETS

In 1956, Andre Norton published her first paperback original. This was CROSSROADS OF TIME, a wild and wooly (and *adult*, not juvenile) cloak-and-dagger romp through parallel futures and alternate Earths. Even on rereading today (it has since been reissued by Ace), it stands up as one of the more enjoyable specimens of rip-roaring "time-opera."

New markets opened up for her material in foreign countries. Books with the Norton byline have since appeared in England, Germany, Italy, France, and Argentina. THE PRINCE COMMANDS had a Danish edition. Germany, in particular, seems to have gone Andre-Norton-mad: at least nine of her novels have been translated and published in that country, including CROSSROADS OF TIME, which did not have a hard-cover edition in this country.

And one of her novels had the rare distinction of being selected for a German book club—SARGASSO OF SPACE, the first of the two 'Solar Queen' books she wrote for Gnome Press under the "Andrew North" byline.

SERIES AND TRILOGIES

Andre Norton began experimenting a little in the 1950's—stretching her literary muscles a bit and limbering up her powers. The first of these stylistic ventures was writing sequels to some of her more outstanding novels, and later she even expanded some of these into trilogies. As the author of two novels about the barbarian hero, Thongor of Lemuria, published by Ace, I know the temptation to follow up one novel with a sequel is well nigh an irresistible one to most writers (after all, the major portion of the inventive work needed for any science or fantasy fiction novel is *background detail and cultural lore* and once you've invented that, it's easy to spin more plots within this pre-completed frame). Publishers, however, and juvenile publishers in particular, tend to shy away from sequels. They think libraries don't like "series" yarns. That her publishers permitted her to turn out sequels galore, is an indication of the popular reception Miss Norton's novels must have received.

For an example of one of her series, let's look briefly at one of her ventures into the field of the time-travel yarn—Miss Norton's 'Time Agent' series. This trilogy started off (with a bang) in THE TIME TRADERS (1958). It continued with GALACTIC DERELICT (1959), and was concluded (we all thought) in THE DEFIANT AGENTS (1962). However, Andre Norton decided to turn this trilogy into the first of her tetralogies, with the publication of a fourth novel in the series, called KEY OUT OF TIME (1963). Now, this particular series is made up of several interweaving plots. One of them is the struggle between the U.S. and the U.S.S.R. to colonize a key planet on the galactic frontier. The gimmick that makes things so lively is briefly stated: because this particular world is a middlin' rugged, wilderness-type world, each side comes up with a clever method of what you might call "temporal regression" on their would-be colonists. They bring up out of each colonist's store of racial memory, the ego of a hardy ancestor from the Good Old Days—the Russkies revert to the Golden Horde of Genghis Khan, and the Americans (who are American Indians) rouse up the spirits of their tough-minded Apache forebears.

Speaking of Amerindians, Andre Norton seems very fond of them in hero-roles for her fiction. She has another series concerning a Navaho named Hosteen Storm. Hosteen's saga opened up with a novel called THE BEAST MASTER in 1959 and continued with 1962's LORD OF THUNDER. If there was a third novel in this very interesting series, I must have overlooked it.

Hosteen's problem is a rather awesome one. His home-world, which is Terra, naturally, has been *destroyed* in a war with the non-humans Xiks. Hosteen gets a job on the frontier planet of Arzor as a member of the Beast Service. He is a natural for this outfit as he has a rare semi-telepathic ability to communicate with animals. In Miss Norton's universe, people with this uncanny skill form man-and-critter scouting teams.

Our hero, Hosteen, is part of a team that consists of Baku the eagle, Surra the dune-cat, and a couple of creatures called Ho and Hing. This subplot of a future man/animal telepathic symbiosis is a favorite device with Andre Norton, and it crops up quite frequently in other books not in this Hosteen Storm series. As a dyed-in-the-fur animal lover myself, I love the idea and wish she'd go into it a bit more deeply.

In my opinion, for what it's worth, these two 'Hosteen Storm' novels are quite possibly her very best science fiction published to date. The boy has genuine human problems to handle, above and beyond the temporary emergencies generated within the structure of her plots. Because of his Navaho ancestry, he feels like an outsider among the predominately Anglo-Saxon colonists. And the feeling of loneliness, or, more properly, alone-ness, this generates in Hosteen is considerably worsened by the helpless feeling of being lost in an alien world, caused by his rootless and wandering life followed since the total destruction of his home planet. His isolation, only partially self-imposed, causes him to draw into an even closer and more intimate relationship with his animal team-mates and lends strong credence to the author's concept of the telepathic/symbiotic animal-man teams used in her future.

In other words, we have in these two novels a rather rare thing in modern science fiction: a very real person with very real problems with which he must learn to cope. And I mean *real* problems, for Hosteen's rootlessness is caused by the destruction of the Earth, which is not an artificial plot-problem which he will be able to circumvent and put straight by the last chapter. This is worlds above and beyond the phoney fictional problems most science fiction heroes are pitted against . . . the O-God-will-we-ever-lick-them-evil-wicked-bad-horrid-monsters-from-Boskone kind of problem.

I find it a mark in her favor, that characters in an Andre Norton novel quite often have credible problems to deal with—problems that do not entirely derive from the science-fictional future of the story, but of the kind and calibre many of us are struggling with today. After all, is Hosteen's trouble particularly different from that of any one of the millions of Displaced Persons rendered homeless—*for good*—by World War II? You just don't expect to find situations of this seriousness and what you might call 'maturity' right smack in the middle of what is, after all, nothing more pretentious than a good juvenile s-f adventure yarn offering fast-action entertainment. More power to her for such as this, says I!

An even more interesting (and probably even more permanently valuable) experiment than merely trilogizing—if there *is* such a word, and I don't think there is—hit the newsstands in 1963. I am referring to one of the best and most important of all the paperback originals Ace Books has published—Andre Norton's rich, brilliant, superbly imaginative and fully adult *pure fantasy* novel, WITCH WORLD.

Frequently in the past, Miss Norton's books have teetered giddily on the razor-thin edge between straight science fiction and full-blooded fantasy. JUDGMENT ON JANUS, for example, was a study in ambiguity: it contained just about as much of a fantasy element as of an element of science. But, with the unexpected publication of WITCH WORLD, Miss Norton took the plunge.

You are probably familiar with the story. If not, by all means read it. The plot is simple: Simon Tregarth, a renegade U.S. Army Colonel goes into a feudal world of magic and mystery by ways devious and strange, which involve a "stone of power" —an ancient magical talisman which Miss Norton labels the "Siege Perilous," and which those who know their *King Arthur* will recognize as the chair Merlin the Magician set up at the Round Table with the warning that only one knight in all the world would sit in it without peril (he was predicting the coming of Sir Galahad, the son of Lancelot du Lac, the knight chosen to achieve the Holy Grail). Well, Tregarth goes into the "Witch World" and gets caught up in the medieval struggle between the three countries of Kolder, Alizon, and Estcarp. This three-way war starts out like a just plain ordinary war, but it soon develops undertones of alien invasion and evil magic, as in the struggle between Gondor and Mordor in THE LORD OF THE RINGS, which was published some years before Miss Norton wrote her splendid WITCH WORLD.

Most people would agree with my estimate that WITCH WORLD is the single best, most "important" and probably most permanent book Andre Norton has written yet. If she is to be remembered and still read by our grand-children, and she has a chance at this mild degree of immortality if she works at it, it will most likely be for WITCH WORLD or something of comparable merit. It's a bloody good yarn, filled with color and excitement, an heroic saga of sorcery and swashbuckling swordplay in the Grande Tradition. The prose is very different and much better than her usual—slower, more thoughtful, polished to a higher gloss, more richly textured and subtly colored. An evocative, even a poetic prose, lightly salted with echoes of Robert E. Howard and the rousing 'Conan' stories. With just a savory hint of J. R. R. Tolkien, and quite a healthy dash of that marvelous Old Master of the fantasy novel, A. Merritt, whom Miss Norton does not list as being among her early loves, along with Burroughs and Ray Cummings, but who probably exerted a formative influence on her work as he did on the writings of Robert E. Howard, Leigh Brackett, Edmond Hamilton, Jack Williamson, Henry Kuttner, Marion Zimmer Bradley, and just about all of us who have specialized in the more adventurous brand of story-telling (yes, on Lin Carter, too).

WITCH WORLD is truly a first-rate job, and if the subsequent publication of WEB OF THE WITCH WORLD and THREE AGAINST THE WITCH WORLD and YEAR OF THE UNICORN have rendered invalid my remark above that this experiment was a more interesting one than "merely writing sequels" I am willing to sacrifice a point in order to have these delightful adult fantasies on my Norton shelf.

Now, back at the beginning of this profile, I mentioned the lack of attention critics and reviewers of science fiction have paid to Miss Norton. When it first became known in the science fiction field that I was doing some research and gathering information towards a brief and informal study of Andre Norton, some people—both readers and, I'm sad to say, a couple of rather "important" professional science fiction writers—asked me why on earth I was wasting time on the work of a writer of "minor or peripheral value, at best." I frankly didn't have a good answer ready at the time. But, while this study was taking shape, I suddenly realized not only why I was interested enough in Andre Norton to study her work, but also why—subconsciously—I knew she was "significant" in the full Lit'ry Critic's sense of the term.

The answer runs something like this. Anyone who has read science fiction at all in a systematic fashion or continuously over a decade or so, knows that science fiction goes by trends or fads of schools of writing. Andre Norton—be she or be she not "minor"—is a good example of a trend that has been growing steadily stronger over the last few years and may, I suspect, be the dominant style of the science fiction of the future.

I will even go a little further, and say that each *decade* in the history of science fiction from the inception of the pulp magazine of s-f in 1926 has been dominated by a single "style" of science fiction story—and that the Andre Norton story may be the dominant style of the 1960s.

Now here's what I mean.

From 1926 to the middle 1930s (roughly speaking), science fiction was under the powerful influence of Hugo Gernsback, who founded the first three magazines devoted entirely to this form of entertainment, *Amazing Stories, Astounding Stories* (now *Analog*, after several title-changes), and *Wonder Stories* (which went through even more title-changes than *Astounding*). Gernsback's trend was towards the gadget. Your typical yarn of that remote and (by me, at least) unlamented era, went something along these lines—and I only exaggerate a little: "Professor Garglezoffter has invented the Electro-Robotic Chicken-Plucker!" —(Sensation.)—"Now the Herr Professor will tell us all exactly how this miraculous new scientific advance *works—*" . . . and he does, for about fifteen thousand very dull words.

Then came the 1940s—the "Golden Forties"—and science fiction fell under (or, more correctly, *rose* under) the guiding hand of John W. Campbell, Jr., editor of ASF. Campbell had an exciting new idea. He would say, in effect, to one of the new writers he was busy discovering (like A. E. Van Vogt, Robert Heinlein, L. Sprague de Camp, Isaac Asimov, James Blish, Clifford D. Simak, L. Ron Hubbard, James H. Schmitz, Henry Kuttner, *et cetera*): "Okay, kid, we grant you your robot chicken-plucker. Forget about giving us a verbal blueprint. Forget about how it works. Just go home and figure out what it would mean to *people*. How would it pose a problem to the now-unemployed *human* chicken-plucker?" And so on. And we got a decade of great and good yarns, still heavy on the technology, but with the *primary emphasis* on human beings and of the impact on their lives made by this or that mechanical marvel.

In the 1950s, a couple of brilliant new magazines called *Galaxy* and *The Magazine of Fantasy & Science Fiction* came along and founded yet another major story-trend. I call this the Pohl-and-Kornbluth story, after the two very able and respected writers who kicked the whole cycle off. Primary emphasis shifted again. Instead of the gadget—instead of the people—writers who followed the path well-beaten by Cyril M. Kornbluth and Frederik Pohl were mostly interested in the society in which a technological advance had occurred. Their stories illustrated how *the culture* was changed by the impact of something new and different. And we had any number of good yarns in which the future (the *near* future) was taken over by advertising men (THE SPACE MERCHANTS)—insurance agencies (PREFERRED RISK)—"senior citizens" (the second part of SEARCH THE SKY)—department stores (HELL'S PAVEMENT)—new religions (MESSIAH, and ELEVENTH COMMANDMENT)—and just about everything, including, somewhere or other, the Garglezoffter Electro-Robotic Chicken-Plucker Corporation. Good stories, too, most of 'em.

But, like all such trends, this one finally wore out and people started looking for something new. And here we are in the 1960s without a single new trend to our name . . . or *are* we?

I wonder. In the last year or two, Ace Books has been publishing a large quantity of a certain kind of story . . . one in which the element of fantasy is intermixed with science fiction. Interplanetary adventure-yarns, in which we have spaceships and magicians simultaneously coexisting, as in Gardner Fox's WARRIOR OF LLARN, Don Wollheim's SWORDSMEN IN THE SKY, Marion Zimmer Bradley's FALCONS OF NARABEDLA, my own THE STAR MAGICIANS, Samuel R. Delany's THE JEWELS OF APTOR and CAPTIVES OF THE FLAME, Andre Norton's four stories of the WITCH WORLD, Henry Kuttner's THE DARK WORLD, Leigh Brackett's PEOPLE OF THE TALISMAN, Ursula K. LeGuin's ROCANNON'S WORLD, Miss Norton's JUDGMENT ON JANUS, Gardner Fox's ARSENAL OF MIRACLES, Robert E. Howard's ALMURIC and others too numerous to mention. They all, every last one of them, combine the elements of fast-action heroics of the sword & sorcery type, with a space or far future or science fictional locale.

And, besides the Howard, Kuttner and Wollheim books above, which are reprints of older stories, we have seen an amazing resurgence of interest in some of the old-time writers of pure fantastic adventure: Ace has done scores of reprints of Edgar Rice Burroughs, Otis Adelbert Kline, Jules Verne, Homer Eon Flint, Ray Cummings, and other writers of this variety. These reprints, to me, at least, indicate a general nostalgia for the lost age of the pulps, for the old fashioned mellerdrammer that we jaded connoisseurs once thought was "corny." And it indicates a general turning-away from the hyper-sophisticated science fiction of the 1950s towards something like the old fashioned adventure story, with trimmings of magic and fantasy, a hearkening back to the rip-roaring kind of science-fantasy, or scientific sword & sorcery, or better yet (if I may coin a phrase that seems to fit the *genre*), a new kind of fiction we might yet be calling *sword & science*.

If this is to be the dominant form of science fiction in the Sixties (and it looks like it from where I'm sitting), we'll see a new brand of science fiction which relies heavily on excitement, adventure, and exotic color, composed of less science and more adventure . . . something, perhaps, like the lead novels we used to see in the wonderful old (and, sadly, long since defunct) magazine, *Planet Stories*. Only, since we have, by and large, a more gifted and experienced crop of writers today, and a more sophisticated audience to write for, the new sword & science yarns will be more adroit and skillful, seasoned with mature and well-conceived imaginative invention.

The kind of fiction I envision as dominant in the 1960s is exemplified by Andre Norton. Her productions to date show this trend in a marked degree: the action-filled adventure science fiction, gradually tending more and more towards pure fantasy, slowly getting further and further from "traditional" adventure s-f and drawing closer and closer to the border between science fiction and straight fantasy, until, at last, she has ventured across this border under full steam. And her recent novels, with their strong primary colors, struck through with "the sense of wonder," with the exotica and strangeness of new planets on the frontiers of the unknown, and with their emphasis on the personal heroism of the characters, illustrates something like what the science fiction of tomorrow may be like.

Prophecy is always a chancy business, and I am well aware I may turn out to be 101% wrong. But all the signs seem to point to a resurgence of the old *Planet Stories* kind of science-fantasy. On this point, I think it's highly significant that Ace Books has been publishing more and more of this kind of fiction in the last couple of years. Ace is, of course, the world's largest and most active science fiction publisher among either hard-cover or paperback houses, and regularly releases *more* science fiction than the other firms put together. And since the "lead" has long since been taken away from the science fiction magazines and gone to the paperbacks, where the best and most "important" fiction of the day is more often than not published *first*, this seems doubly significant.

If my attempt at a qualified prediction turns out to be correct, and Andre Norton is a pivotal figure and a prime example of the kind of interplanetary fantasy I see coming up big for this decade, then we can trace in her books alone this trend. STAR MAN'S SON is straight adventure science fiction. JUDGMENT ON JANUS is mostly fantasy, but laid against a science fiction backdrop. WEB OF THE WITCH WORLD is almost pure fantasy, with only touches of science fiction in the background.

Andre Norton may be riding the crest of the wave of the future. But, in any case, I wish her well.